UNDER THE SKY

LILIZ BLACK

To my supporters,
Your belief turned dreams into chapters.
We made it.

Playlist:

"Beautiful Things"- Benson Boone
"Dangerously"- Charlie Puth
"Bite"- D.O
"Love me like that"- Sam Kim
"Scent"- Sam Kim
"The Reason of my Smiles"- Seventeen
"Hold me Back"- Heize

1
INTRODUCTIONS

I glanced at the empty document on my computer screen, the cursor flickering angrily as if parading my incapacity for writing. Forty-five minutes later, I hadn't typed a single word. My emotions tangled, a tight sensation gripped my chest, and I felt completely useless for the current work. Melancholic, romantic music slowly played from my headphones, now lying on my neck, aggravating my sadness even more.

Love was what my heart craved; the romance stories I had been reading heightened that need. These stories of damsels in crisis meeting their destined partner and enjoying wonderful romance made me hollow and afraid. Was it my poor judgment of character, always selecting the wrong person to share my life with, or were Korean dramas to blame for this distorted view of love?

People tell us these tales are only fiction, that such events never really occur in daily life. But as I looked through social media, I couldn't help but see innumerable pictures and tales of others, joyful and in love, celebrating life while I stayed stuck in my routine. Years had gone by since my previous outing with a former high school classmate. I had lost touch with most of my former classmates; I often go back to my world, seeking a pleasant place within myself.

Although it's now a useless achievement, I had earned a degree in graphic design. Cheap foreign freelancers from other countries dominated the low-paying job path in my area. This situation drove me to move to Montana, where I eventually found work as a strategy coordinator in the marketing division, far from my dream field.

I met my boyfriend at the end of my university degree, and together after one year we decided to move to Montana in search of new opportunities. It was all beautiful at first. However, as time passed, the initial excitement faded, and a monotonous routine took control. He ate, slept, and withdrew to his studio; I cleaned, cooked, and did the dishes. Our relationship seemed more like those of closest friends or roommates than of lovers. Although that may sound unpleasant, it reflects the reality of our situation.

Living with him was acceptable at first, but the reality of the situation set in quickly. I started looking after another person in addition to myself. While he looked indifferent about my efforts, I cleaned, cooked, and oversaw the home tasks. Joy defines the nature of a connection. It's about delight in seeing each other, in talking, in sharing, and in making love. But today our relationship feels dead and boring. Knowing I would have to resolve messes, figure out meals, and tidy up before finally withdrawing to my refuge, I hated returning home after work.

My refuge was a place where I could bury myself in books, plays, games, and writing. My headset helped me to block out the surroundings and enter my own small universe. Every day felt the same. Every time he wanted sex, he would come to me, and I would comply, hoping for a brief respite. Still, my mind kept returning to the "what-ifs" and "should haves" that tormented earlier decisions.

Now here I was, alone, without friends, gazing at my screen, striving to create something worthwhile. My partner felt as though he was only a passenger in my life, and my work caused continual stress. Despite my profound understanding that my longing was merely a fantasy, I yearned for someone to lift me out of this dreariness.

Once a site of adventure and opportunity, the house felt like a prison. The traces of unmet dreams seemed to permeate every place. The walls, now teasing me with their vivid colors and strong lines, were covered in posters of the graphic designs I had dreamed of producing, a sharp contrast to the grayness that had crept into my existence.

Often, I would find myself peering out the window at the world beyond—a world that seemed so vivid and alive. However, everything felt stagnant within these walls. The routine was intolerable now. The morning rush, which included the flurry of preparing breakfast, the boredom of project reports, and the solemn dinners, left few words and even fewer emotions.

Once a place where I experimented with new dishes and enjoyed cooking, the kitchen now felt like a battlefield. The sight of dirty dishes stacked in the sink made my shoulders seem heavier. I used to take immense satisfaction in keeping the house tidy, but it seemed like an endless cycle of mess and cleanup, reflecting the messiness of my emotions.

Not even my little haven, the book-filled, game-filled room with my writing desk, could offer the comfort it used to. The words failed to flow, and the stories that used to flow naturally felt hollow and forced now. For hours, I would sit there with the cursor blinking on a blank screen, a quiet reminder of my creative block.

The silence was intolerable at night as I lay in bed. The quiet snores of my boyfriend next to me had little effect in filling the gap. I yearned for deep talks and a relationship transcending appearances. Every attempt I made to express my emotions, however, met with either apathy or a swift change in subject. It seemed like we were living in different universes, as our lives only crossed during fleeting and superficial moments.

The gloom of the room seems to reflect the gloom in my emotions. The squandered opportunities, the misguided routes, and the aspirations that now seem so distant haunt me. Haunted me with "what ifs" and "should haves," they sap tranquility and sleep.

I realized that I needed to act. Trapped in a circle of misery and discontent, I could not carry on living this way. Still, the idea of acting or deviating from this pattern was scary. It meant facing my anxieties, the unknown, and maybe having to make difficult decisions. It required owning my discontent and realizing things had to be different.

For now, though, I stayed immobilized by doubt and anxiety. The days melted together, each one a repeat of the last. As I glanced at the blank document on my computer screen, with the cursor blinking impatiently, I couldn't help but worry whether I would ever find the bravery to break free and pursue the happiness I desperately want.

****

Rang, RANG, RANG.

The sound made me sigh. My hand stumbled over the blankets, looking for my phone in the darkness. At last, I felt the firm surface of my phone and grabbed it.

I sighed, half-opened my eyes, and checked the time. It was five thirty-two AM. Last night, I had online Korean classes and stayed up late studying. My day was just starting, and I already hated the extended hours until I could close my eyes and separate from this planet.

I looked across at the opposite side of the bed. It was empty, as usual. I've spent yet another night alone. Owen must be doing his thing in his study. He would play with his online friends or read graphic novels during sleepless nights.

Turning off the alert, I rose up and began getting ready for the day ahead, neglecting the lethargy dragging down my body. I was the one working primarily. Typically, I accepted double shifts and extra hours, often working ten to twelve hours each day to earn enough money to cover household expenses.

My work was demanding, painful, and irritating. I had to assist others, sometimes dinosaurs, in comprehending and articulating how reports and technology worked. I started working as a customer agent in a call center. I was promoted to the marketing department as a strategy coordinator of IME Enterprises after developing such strong organizational and presentation skills. Among the largest suppliers of computers, phones, and everything smart-activated out there is IME Enterprises.

Although the position is not directly related to my field of study, it has allowed me to apply skills that are relevant to my degree.

I would get up in the morning to work out and get breakfast and lunch ready for us both. Although Owen, my boyfriend, worked for the same company, his shifts were shorter than mine because he was a sales agent on the store floor. But today I was too exhausted to work out, and by eight AM it was already too late to accomplish both.

I knocked at his study door after preparing breakfast. "Breakfast is ready."

Scrolling around social media or reading a short narrative, I quickly left to bathe and eat my breakfast. By the time I finished, Owen would come out to grab his meal. His light brown wavy hair as though he had just swept his hands through it in a flash of insight. Through his thin-framed glasses, his gentle hazel gaze locked on me. Usually, his eyes would hide behind the reflecting surface of his spectacles, making emotional interpretation challenging. But this time, he just grinned as he picked up his plate, naked while wearing his headset, and made his way back to his cave.

He exuded an undercurrent of concentration and drive, especially when immersed in his work in the study, despite his laid-back appearance. He likes to hum gently, a random tune usually joining him to produce a strange but familiar background noise in our apartment.

"I need to get there at eight today!" I replied, "Do I need to take an Uber, or will you be able to drive me?"

The trouble arose from having only one car and our differing schedules. His lack of accountability creates significant problems for me in getting to work on time. Owen always excelled in sales and brought in profit; hence, the manager let him be late for his shifts.

At 7:30, he was at last getting ready to drive me to work. His usual attire consisted of simple trousers, a T-shirt, and perhaps a flannel shirt thrown over them, embodying a comfortable mix of practicality and apathy towards fashion. The journey was agonizingly silent. He was singing a song through his earbud, while I lost myself in my phone, scrolling through the daily fresh emails.

"See you," I murmured as he stopped in front of my building to gather his stuff. "I'll call once I'm done."

"Sure. "Love you," he answered. I froze in surprise and turned to look at him.

"Love you too?" Uncertain about what to expect, I responded. I inhaled deeply and turned to face my second hell, that of work.

The workplace smelled like antiseptic as I walked into the building. The strong brightness of the fluorescent lights highlights the clean surroundings I would be facing. With a laptop computer, a headset, and stacks of paperwork appearing to get bigger every day, I nestled inside my cubicle, the little area filled with instruments of my profession.

The hours passed, each call merging into the next to create a boring loop of technical problems and complaints. The sheer weight of the chores that needed my attention eclipsed the fleeting gratification I felt when I solved an issue. With every minute that went by, my vitality was dwindling, and I could feel tiredness pushing down on me.

Lunch presented a fleeting break. With one hand holding a meal and my phone in the other, I sat in the break room surfing social media. The pictures of friends and acquaintances leading apparently flawless lives just made me feel more alone. I yearned for the link and happiness they seemed to share so naturally.

The afternoon produced more of the same: emails and spreadsheets. I also received calls, but my mind wandered as ideas about Owen floated back to me. Our relationship has become a daily ritual devoid of the spark and passion we previously possessed. I asked whether he shared my sentiments or if he was pleased with the current situation.

2
COFFEE & CHOCOLATE

8:04 PM

I sighed as I checked my watch. I had my bag and lunch bag with me as I stood in front of my office building, looking out at the street, trying to decide whether to call Owen to come get me or just go to the closest bar and have a drink.

At work, the day had been exceedingly difficult. With the arrival of new interns, we had to balance our workload with theirs. The upper management was twice as demanding, and everyone was tense and antagonistic. I attempted to adjust the new interns to their tasks and surroundings for most of the day.

I chose to go down the street to one of the bars that served food. I would rather not return home to work again. As I frequented the place for some lunch or late dinners, the bartender greeted me warmly.

"Fancy seeing you here, Liliam."

I placed my stuff on the stool next to me and leaned my head down on the bar. "The usual."

The bartender laughed, massaging his black mustache. Tom has been in this bar for as long as I can remember. He always had a smile and playful dark brown eyes, and his wavy dark hair was slicked back, likely to conceal the bald spot developing at the center of his head. "Coming right up."

He yelled my usual order to the boy in the kitchen. Then, he opened a Michelob and placed it beside my face, resting on the cold surface of the bar. "On the house, missy. You seem to need it."

I thanked him with a smile. "Work was hectic. I don't even want to go back home yet."

"Understandable. We've all been there."

"Thank you, Tom." I took the cold beer and drank the bitter yet refreshing liquid.

As I did, the hairs on the back of my neck prickled and stood up. It was that familiar feeling you get when someone is watching you intently. I shifted my weight, pulled my long black hair free from its ponytail, and took a breath.

Through the usual aroma of food coming from the kitchen, I picked up something different—something peculiar.

In a place like Melvin's Pub, the smell of coffee and chocolate was unusual. These kinds of places usually reek of beer, grease, and—if crowded—sweat. However, this aroma was intense, dominating all other sensations and causing my mouth to ache with longing. You know that feeling you experience when you're thirsty for something. Coffee has always been a calming scent for me, but this time, it was electric—exhilarating—sending shivers down my spine.

Still, the prickling sensation at the back of my neck wouldn't leave. I finally turned, scanning the room. My amber eyes locked onto a figure in the far corner of the room, and my breath caught.

He sat like sin wrapped in denim, one leg crossed lazily over the other, a bottle of beer resting on the ankle of his boot. His other arm draped across the booth's top edge; muscles flexed just enough to show power in restraint. His forearms were inked—bold tribal designs that trailed up, disappearing beneath the rolled sleeves of his gray button-up. The first few buttons were undone, revealing a glimpse of sun-kissed skin and the stark lines of his chest.

His jawline could've cut glass—sharply defined, framed by a perfectly trimmed beard that only added to the raw masculinity of his face. Tousled dark hair curled slightly over his ears, like he'd just run his fingers through it after something reckless.

But it was his eyes that undid me.

Emerald. Bright and burning.

He was staring—at me. He appeared to understand every aspect of my appearance.

Heat licked up my spine, and I dropped my gaze fast, heart pounding. My cheeks flamed, and something low in my belly tightened.

I clutched my beer like it might anchor me, but my skin buzzed with awareness. Goosebumps rippled across me, and that familiar ache curled deep and low. I could feel his stare, even with my eyes down, and it was doing dangerous things to my body.

God, he looked like every forbidden fantasy I'd ever had.

All sharp edges and slow fire.

He was the kind of man who wouldn't ask permission to ruin you—he'd just do it… and make you thank him for it.

Snap out of it. I cursed myself silently, dragging my gaze back to the beer in front of me. My deprived brain might have been deceiving me.

Tom returned with my food, offering a polite nod as he placed the plate down. I thanked him, forcing my attention onto my steak quesadilla and trying to ignore the way the scent of coffee and chocolate was growing thicker and richer—like it was coming alive in the air around me.

I took one bite. Then I felt it.

His presence.

That scent—fresh-brewed coffee laced with dark chocolate—swept over me like a warm breath against my neck. My stomach flipped. A chair scraped against the floor beside me, and a shadow filled the seat next to mine.

Oh, God.

He was here.

If you're a coffee lover, you know that moment. The first inhale of freshly brewed warm coffee after a long, brutal day. It is a moment of calm, euphoric release. Now imagine that scent wrapped around a man who looked like sin—and that scent wasn't in a cup; it was him.

It hit me so hard I had to bite down on my tongue to stop myself from leaning in—smelling him. I could feel those eyes before I even looked. Green. He was observing me as if I were a treasure to cherish.

I looked up slowly, the quesadilla pausing halfway to my lips, and I froze.

He was sitting beside me. Our bodies were separated by a mere five inches of air. From this close, I could see everything. I could see the warm honey tone of his sun-kissed skin. The slight stubble traced his sharp jaw. Those goddamn emerald eyes glinted as if they already knew how I would taste.

Heat curled through me like smoke. Deep. Low. Dangerous.

I didn't get like this. Ever. A glance didn't intimidate me. Lust had never been my driving force. But this man...this scent...was unraveling something I didn't even know existed inside me.

It was hunger. Raw. Wild.

And it terrified me.

In that instant, I desired to disregard politeness and immerse my face in his chest, absorbing every detail of him until I dissolved. To trail my fingers along the hard ridges of his body, memorizing every sculpted inch as if it were sacred scripture. I want to shape myself into his body, pressing against his skin and inhaling deeply until the space between us vanishes.

He seems older. Not significantly older—perhaps five or six years—but his presence was palpable when he gazed at me.

I dropped my gaze to my plate and muttered under my breath, "Please, brain. Don't do this."

"Please, what?"

He had a rich, velvety, gravelly voice. I felt a shock go right through me. I looked up in surprise as he drew closer, bringing us closer with calm, purposeful determination.

His words caught in my throat as I was biting into a quesadilla. Panicked, I began coughing until I felt his warm, solid hand against my back.

Oh, hell.

The second his fingers touched me, the heat flared beneath my skin like an open flame, sending a shiver racing down my spine. It curled down my abdomen, a slow, aching coil of want that pulsed deep in my core.

"Are you okay?" He murmured, his voice brushing the shell of my ear.

I nodded quickly, reaching for my beer with trembling fingers and taking a long gulp to steady myself. "Yeah. Sorry."

But his hand didn't move.

It stayed, resting at the base of my spine, possessive and intimate like we were already something more. His touch burned there, and I wasn't sure I ever wanted it to go.

He smiled then. Slow. Dreamy. Devastating. It was the kind of smile that made you feel dizzy.

My heart fluttered.

"Do—do I know you?" I managed to speak, but my voice came out too breathy and too soft.

"I wish you did," he said, his tone dark with something deeper. His fingers drifted from my lower back, up my arm, brushing the sensitive skin of my forearm, until they found my hand—the one still holding my food.

Before I could react, he leaned in and took a small bite from the quesadilla, his lips brushing my knuckles. His emerald eyes never left mine.

My breath caught.

He was so close now, I could taste the scent of him—coffee, dark chocolate, and heat. It filled my lungs and made my thoughts dissolve. My pulse thundered, wild and uncontained.

The scene would have been unsettling with any other man at any other moment. However, with him, the situation was different.

There was something magnetic, undeniable, about him. He exerted a force that defied reason and softened my knees.

"Zeff Gunnolf," he said, his voice smooth and rich as sin. His fingers brushed my forearm—light, deliberate, and impossibly gentle for a man built like him. Despite being muscle-bound and sharp-edged, his touch felt like silk against my skin.

Or perhaps I was the only one fantasizing.

"Liliam," I breathed. "Liliam Black."

His gaze locked with mine—those piercing green eyes drinking me in like I was already his. The intoxicating scent of dark coffee and chocolate curled around me, making my thoughts swim. I could barely remember where I was, let alone the half-eaten quesadilla on my plate.

He reached out, slowly and sensually, and curled his fingers around mine, pulling my hand away from the counter, from reality. My breath hitched.

Then—his lips.

They kissed me so tenderly and respectfully that it burned my knuckles. The contact ignited every nerve in my body with a blast of heat. My cheeks began to flush hot, my fingers burned from the thought of his kiss, and my heart pounded in my ears.

But worse, my core clenched. My core tightened with a raw, aching need that startled me.

I should've pulled away.

I didn't.

I couldn't.

Something about his hand—his warmth—his presence—kept me tethered. Perhaps it was the way his eyes clung to me, ensnaring me as if his gravitational pull held me.

Was it the heat of his touch?

Or the raw power of this man, who made me feel more with a kiss on my fingers than anyone ever had with their whole body?

And God help me… I didn't want it to stop.

"Don't you know how to answer your phone?"

The voice snapped me back to reality. I quickly pulled my hand away and turned to find Owen standing in the doorway, throwing me an annoyed glance. He was wearing his usual attire—a T-shirt, shorts, and flip-flops.

I must have left my phone on Do Not Disturb. I glanced down at my bag, and sure enough, three missed calls glared back at me from the screen.

"I'm sorry—"

"Hurry!"

My eyes drifted back to the man, Zeff, and I nearly jumped. He continued to watch, his gaze now fixed on Owen, his expression dark and unreadable. His eyes… they were no longer green.

They were black.

His muscles were tense, his jaw clenched, and a low growl rumbled from his chest.

Wait, when did his eyes change?

"Nice meeting you, Zeff," I said quickly, forcing a smile as I turned and followed Owen to the car.

But as I walked away, my entire body hesitated. The scent of coffee and chocolate lingered behind me, seductive and impossible to ignore. It wrapped around me like a tether, tempting me to look back.

I didn't.

With a heavy sigh, I shook the feeling off and followed my partner into the hellhole I called home.

3
THE MATE

Zeff

Anyone can say what they want, but for me, the best fruit is blackberries. They have a complex and rich flavor, offering a sweet yet tart taste with earthy undertones, often accompanied by a subtle hint of acidity. The juiciness adds to their appeal, providing a burst of flavor with every bite. While many choose the same old strawberries, for me, it has always been blackberries.

Since childhood, my mother would plant blackberry bushes, and I would often sneak out to harvest the fresh fruit at its ripest, enjoying the tart flavor. The memory of those sun-warmed berries, their deep purple juice staining my fingers, is a cherished part of my past. Blackberries have always been a comforting, nostalgic delight, a small but profound pleasure in my life.

By the time I reached seventeen, as is customary for every adolescent in our community, we encountered our wolf. Given to us by our ancestors and our god to guide the family in the traditions of our early roots, it is then that we become men and shift into our inner selves. Everything was easier for kids in Darwood Reservoir, except when you were an Alpha.

When you are born into a line of Alphas, there are more responsibilities involved. A leader's den welcomes you into its fold and shapes you into a leader as you mature. You are towered and crowned with the title and responsibilities of an Alpha. You must lead the pack, convey peace around us, and eliminate threats that might sway the roots our ancestors have built. We are a supernatural paradigm of order and power, and many look up to the packs of the Wolves.

Life is a cycle. We meet our wolf; two years later, we are ready to meet our mate for life, with whom we would build a family, help the companies, and contribute to the community. But we Alphas are different. My upbringing as the son of a king's general prepared me for war. My upbringing instilled tactics, strength, and a profound understanding of history. As the only heir, it was my duty to learn and lead the next generation of Darwood into prosperity. We receive training to prepare us for potential challenges that could threaten our status. A lack of a mate can subdue that status.

Meeting your mate feels like a gravitational pull that draws you towards them. Our mates serve as our anchors, provide balance, and complete the harmony of a well-balanced wolf. You don't choose it. Nature does. And when it does, you will know by the smell and the aura emitted.

I have always yearned for that smell, and I am confident it will be the scent of blackberries. Today marks my twenty-sixth year, and I am still waiting for that mate to come.

The Gunnolf bloodline has always been one of the strongest, among the last to carry the near-extinct blood of the Lycans. Before tradition changed, we were the last lineage to hold the throne. For my grandfather, that change was a relief.

He no longer had to carry the weight of a crown steeped in blood, not after his father plunged the packs into war in a frenzy for power. The council stripped him of his title and abolished the hereditary rule.

For the past century, I've taken part in the new tradition—an open trial held every ten years to choose a king. I never sought the crown myself, but the King's Council requires that every Alpha from each pack participate.

Although I have not yet found my mate, my parents have grown restless in their search for the Luna who will lead both my pack and our family's companies. Many have questioned my status, but I have prevailed. I have roamed all over the reservoir and visited other packs, looking for my mate, but I have not found anyone yet.

Josh, my best friend and beta in command, suggested I go out and explore the humans. While it's uncommon for us to find mates in the human world, my hopes were dwindling to find one among my kind.

The idea that someone from outside could become Luna has made my parents somewhat sad over the years. They suggested designating another suitor as a possible mate, in line with other customs. Although the attraction may not be as nature intended, it fulfills the purpose of having a Luna within the pack and ensuring the continuation of our generations.

The elder of our pack, Greyfur, was against it. Gifted with the Third Sight, the ability to glimpse the future through dreams, he believed my destined mate would bring greatness. So here I am, eight years later, still waiting impatiently.

The arrival of the Parr complicates matters significantly. It's an animal instinct to elope—wolves experience it in different seasons, driven by nature's call to grow the pack. It manifests as an intense heat and a powerful yearning for sexual release.

Many wolves spend it with their mates; others choose unmated partners to ease the tension. Still, many people say that the Parr is significantly more intense when it is shared with one's fated mate.

The first time was suffocating. It was a blazing, consuming heat, an endless battle for control. For an Alpha, it's ten times stronger. While young wolves often spend their first three years overwhelmed by pleasure, for me, it was more torture than indulgence. I am an Alpha, a figure of status, and I ended up eloping with partners carefully chosen by my mother. She wished to prevent the future Alpha from becoming involved with a mated individual.

We do not condone sexual intercourse with a mated individual. When wolves mate, a unique bond forms that ties their emotions and moods together. Betraying that bond, causes pain to the chosen mate and is considered disloyalty to the gods.

Some wolves have used this loophole to deliberately hurt their mates during fights, acts of revenge, or rejections. The abuse became so severe that the King's Council and Pack Council had to step in, issuing laws to punish those who weaponized the bond for cruelty. Human mates, however, are different. They don't experience the bond until they receive a marking.

Rejection carries its pain. However, if the rejection is mutual, it heals more quickly and allows for a second mating. Nature always allows a second chance. That's why the Elder discouraged arranged markings. He believed nature should decide the bond.

I learned to tame the Parr rhythm, transforming it from a wildfire to a slow burn simmering beneath the surface. By twenty-two, I stopped entertaining my mother's carefully chosen partners. It no longer made sense to silence the ache with borrowed bodies.

It unsettled my father. *An Alpha*, he said, *must never deny the call of instinct.* But I was weary of ceremony. My soul hungered for the fulfillment of expectations.

How could I keep feasting on second plates when I knew somewhere my feast was still out there, waiting?

My wolf understood. He yearned for that connection. When the Parr hits, I would find myself in my wolf form, deep in the woods of Blue Mountain, desperately looking for the smell of blackberries.

****

I glanced down at my phone, waiting for Josh to answer my last message.

Chill, man. I'm finishing something here. I'll be down soon. Could I remind you that I'm protecting you while you roam around?

Josh was my beta and my best friend. His family had served the Gunnolfs for generations, so we grew up like brothers, despite our frequent disagreements.

"You suggested this," I replied.

You must find your mate, my friend. Derion's getting pushy with the council.

I know that.

I took a long pull from my beer, jaw tightening. Eight years of waiting had started to raise flags, and now the council was circling like vultures. A group of ancient wolves, deeply rooted in tradition, was also present. Derion was already attempting to convince them of his superiority, highlighting his mated status as if he were the successor to Fenrir.

I set the phone down with a dull thud and leaned back in the booth, exhaling sharply through my nose. He wasn't wrong. But fuck him.

My family had bled for this pack. They had defended these lands long before Derion ever let out his first cry. Now, as the Parr drew nearer, I could sense its presence beneath my skin and in my bones. The agitation. The hunger. There was an increasing sense of need.

Josh had picked the spot: Marvin's Pub. It was one of his regular haunts. The owner was a friend, and the place sat in the middle of an urban strip, always packed with people. Josh called it "good exposure."

I called it a damn headache.

I didn't mind being around humans, but their stares made me uncomfortable. They made my skin itch. I wasn't exactly inconspicuous, a six-foot wall of muscle, tribal ink running down my arms and up my neck, carved with the markings of the Darwood Reservoir wolves. Most locals had heard of us. Indigenous. Sacred. Territorial. Strong. They were the ones who strolled through the forests as the moon reached its peak.

I also wore clothing that did not blend into the background.

Worn jeans, mountain boots still dusted from my morning run, and a charcoal-gray button-down rolled up to my elbows—casual but fitted to my build. My forearms, inked and tense, rested against the dark wood of the booth. The tattoo that curled from my wrist to my bicep pulsed slightly as I shifted an old symbol of protection and power.

However, some people whispered different ideas in the darkness, cautioning us to tread carefully before the truth shattered everything wide open.

My wolf, Gaius, was impossible today. He was skulking just under my skin, growling and huffing with each breath, his impatience piercing my last forbearance.

"Stop it, Gaius."

"Need mate," he growled back, his voice low and aching.

"You think I don't know that?"

But the conversation ended the moment the door opened, and *she* walked in.

She moved with the quiet fatigue of someone freshly unburdened from a long day, shoulder bag slipping lower with every step, a lunch tote swinging lightly at her side. Her skin was porcelain, untouched by sunlight, smooth and pale like moonlight poured into human form. It only heightened the contrast of her figure, an unapologetic hourglass shape wrapped in a fitted black pencil skirt that kissed every curve of her hips with reverence.

The crisp white blouse she wore clung softly to her chest, the faint strain of fabric around her bust hinting at tension, with one button left undone, not from carelessness but from the kind of subtle defiance only someone exhausted and sensual could wear with ease.

Her black hair was drawn up into a high ponytail, polished but not rigid, the strands falling in soft waves that danced just between restraint and temptation, trailing like silk down the line of her spine. She didn't need to try. She was the kind of woman who walked into a room and made you forget what you were doing.

She made it to the bar and dropped her things with a soft sigh, sinking into the stool like she was melting into it. Then she leaned forward, resting her head gently on her folded arms.

Mate.

Gaius howled.

I watched as she murmured a thank-you to Tom, the bartender, accepting her beer. And then…

She pulled out the hair tie.

Her dark hair unraveled in a slow cascade, falling like silk down her back. And that's when it hit me.

Blackberries.

Sweet, juicy, and tantalizing, the aroma swept over me in waves. My lips virtually watered from the primordial memory it evoked, and my lungs soaked it in.

Gaius moaned and sniffed hard before letting out a deep, victorious growl.

Here.

My gaze swept the pub instinctively, but it always came back to her. She wore a pencil skirt and blouse. She was the only one who exuded a scent reminiscent of heaven and home.

A human.

She slowly scanned the room, and then her eyes met mine.

She met me with two sweet, innocent amber eyes.

My grip tightened on the edge of the booth, fighting against the magnetic pull that practically yanked me forward. Every cell in my body yearned to move, to claim, to mark. Her gaze lingered on me, curious, unaware of the storm she'd just ignited.

She didn't feel it. Not yet. Humans rarely did until they were marked. But I knew.

I fucking knew it.

She was mine.

And the only thing standing between me and her was the leash I barely had in my control. My wolf was frantic—scratching, pacing, pushing against my ribs like he could burst free and claim her right there in the middle of the damn bar.

"Gaius, settle! She's human; you'll scare her!"

He growled in protest, a guttural sound that rumbled through my bones.

Her breath hitched. And she blushed, looking away.

Gaius whimpered as if someone had touched him, as if her reaction had penetrated his chest and tightened it.

"Felt," he whispered. She felt something.

And then—

Move.

I didn't even think. My body obeyed.

I was clutching the booth one moment, and then I was standing up and pacing the room like somebody under the influence of hunger. It was only when I was right there, slipping onto the stool next to her, that she noticed.

She glanced up mid-bite, startled. Her eyes widened, and she stopped chewing, lips parting in surprise. She looked so soft. So real. The tip of her tongue peeked out as if to catch the sour cream near the corner of her mouth, and my entire focus narrowed to that tiny gesture.

I wanted to lean in.

Taste it.

Taste *her*.

"Please, brain, stop it," she muttered under her breath.

She had no idea I could hear her.

I leaned down, my voice low and close. "Please, what?"

She jolted. Adorably startled, her quesadilla betrayed her, catching in her throat. Her body tensed in panic, and I moved without hesitation. My hand slid across her back, firm and comforting, as I tapped between her shoulders.

The moment I touched her, everything ignited.

Even through the thin cotton of her blouse, I could feel the heat of her skin. She exuded a hum that transcended mere humanity. Her warmth seeped into my palm, and my fingers itched to explore more of her spine, her neck, and the dip of her lower back.

She coughed, nodded, and took a sip of beer, and my hand stayed.

I didn't intend to. However, I felt grounded as her body leaned gently against mine.

"Are you okay?" I asked, voice lower than intended.

She nodded again, cheeks flushed, eyes wide. Her breath was shallow. Her fingers trembled ever so slightly around her glass.

She felt it.

Even if she didn't know what it was yet, her body did.

She nodded and took a long gulp of her beer. "Yes, sorry."

I allowed my hand to remain where it was resting lightly on her back. Enjoy it. A low throb of longing went right to my stomach as her warmth seeped into my palm and through the thin cloth.

God, I wanted this. I wanted her.

"Do—do I know you?" She asked, her voice a little unsteady, her lips slightly parted from the drink.

"I wish I did," I said, my voice lower now, husky with the weight of everything I was holding back. My fingers slipped from her back, tracing down the curve of her arm, over the soft skin of her forearm until they reached her hand, her delicate fingers still holding the quesadilla.

I didn't hesitate.

I leaned in and took a bite from it, right from her hand—my mouth brushing the spot where hers had been. The heat of her skin and the taste of her lips lingering on the food, and her closeness all felt like torture. My body reacted instantly, a tight coil of want winding through me, and my throat worked to swallow more than just the bite.

Her scent of blackberries and warmth flooded me and was addictive. I wanted to drown in it. My pulse throbbed in my neck, my grip tightening slightly around her hand as I breathed her in.

Her breath hitched. Her heart pounded.

She felt it.

Goddess, her reactions are killing me.

"Zeff Gunnolf," I murmured, as my fingers finally brushed the soft inside of her wrist to feel her skin there. My voice almost trembled from restraint. For a human, she radiated such heat. Normally, our kind ran hotter than theirs, but with her? She exuded an uncontrollable intensity.

And for a sick, fleeting second, my brain offered up an image—her bare skin against mine, her warmth pressed to me, begging to be devoured.

I nearly groaned. I felt my groin harden.

"Liliam," she whispered. "Liliam Black."

The way she said it—breathless, hesitant, enchanted—was lethal.

I gently took her hand in mine, lifting it slowly away from the forgotten food. I guided her fingers to my lips and kissed them softly, reverently, achingly.

My eyes never left hers. I needed her to feel it. The heat. The claim. The pull was impossible to resist.

When my lips touched her skin, a jolt surged through me like lightning, and Gaius roared in my head.

Mark her. Take her. Ours.

I wanted to.

Indeed, I wanted to push the chairs aside and hold her against the bar. But I stayed motionless, shivering beneath the surface, the pain too great. She did not withdraw. But I held still, trembling under the surface, drowning in the ache.

She didn't pull away.

So, I didn't let go.

"Don't you know how to answer your phone?"

The voice snapped me back to reality. She pulled her hand away, turning toward the male now standing in the entrance, his tone sharp, his gaze annoyed. He wore a t-shirt, shorts, and flip-flops—casual, careless, and completely oblivious to what he'd just interrupted.

My wolf growled. A swift breath caught in my throat as my muscles tensed, coiled tight with instinct.

Who the hell was this fucker barking at her like that?

"I'm sorry—" she began.

"Hurry!"

My eyes locked on him, dark with fury. My nostrils flared, my wolf, Gaius, rising hot beneath my skin like smoke from a wildfire.

Easy, Gaius. We're in human territory, I warned, barely holding the line. But the growl escaped anyway, low and dangerous.

I knew my eyes had shifted. My wolf's darkness was showing now.

"Nice meeting you, Zeff," she said, trying for a smile as she turned to follow the male back to the car.

My wolf whined, claws scraping inside me. She was walking away, leaving us. And everything inside me pulled toward her like a magnet, desperate for the heat of her skin, the scent of blackberries, and the sound of her breath.

She paused. She hesitated momentarily.

And for that one, fragile heartbeat, I thought she might turn back. But she didn't. With a heavy sigh, she shook her head and followed him.

And just like that, she was gone.

4
THE WOLF

Liliam

"Why didn't you call?"

I stared at my hand resting on my knees as the car sped through the streets. Owen's anger radiated off him like waves of heat, thickening the already suffocating air in the vehicle. His grip on the steering wheel was iron-tight, knuckles white, and every turn he took was too sharp, every acceleration too fast.

"I just wanted some time alone—"

"With somebody?"

His words cut through the air like a slap. I flinched, glancing at him. He clenched his jaw, his eyes fixed on the road, seething.

"No! I went to eat and have a beer. He sat next to me; that's all."

"Kissing your hand? Eating without me?"

"Jesus, Owen! You're a grown man! You know how to use a stove."

My tone was more direct than I had intended, yet I was wary of treading carefully. Still, it only fueled the fire.

"Why was he kissing your hand, Liliam?" His voice was low, tight with accusation.

"I don't know! It was. It was part of the introduction—"

He scoffed, bitter and mocking. "What, is he from the 1800s now?"

I folded my arms, feeling the weight of his jealousy press against my chest like a stone.

"Think whatever the hell you want."

"You were in a bar with another man, ignoring my calls. What am I supposed to think?"

I didn't answer. I turned to the window, watching the city blur by—just color and noise and static now. Silence clawed its way into the car, cold and consuming.

When we pulled into the driveway, neither of us said a word. The click of the front door sounded like a gunshot in the quiet. I opened the door and walked into the house, straight to the bathroom.

I closed the door behind me and pressed my back against it, the cool wood grounding me for a fleeting moment. My chest was tight, and my breath was shallow.

Then I heard it: the studio door slamming shut.

Loud. Violent. My knees gave out, and I slid to the floor, arms wrapped around myself. Tears slipped silently down my cheeks, falling onto the tile as the soft buzz of the bathroom light hummed overhead.

I didn't know how much more I could take.

When will this end?

****

I was never fond of forests. Where others saw peace and serenity, I saw bug bites and tangled hair. The outdoors, to me, was a theater of extremes—heat or cold, buzzing mosquitoes, and too many things with legs. With my pale skin, nature's predators could have easily mistaken me for a walking dessert tray.

And yet...

Some part of me always drifted back to the woods.

The verdant surroundings captivated me. The hush. The hush echoed with the pulse of something more ancient than memory.

So, when I found myself in a dense forest, I wasn't surprised.

The canopy above fractured the moonlight into silver ribbons that danced over the earth. The air was cool and crisp, laced with the scent of moss and pine. My footsteps were light, almost ghostly, as I moved through the underbrush, running.

I didn't know what. All I knew was that I had to run.

My heart pounded like a drumbeat of warning, adrenaline flooding my limbs.

The trees blurred as I picked up speed, breath hitching in sharp, ragged bursts. Behind me. I felt it.

A sense of dread crept in. That sense of primal alertness was palpable. Something was following me.

The shadows moved as if they had teeth. They wrapped around my path, whispering threats I couldn't see. Panic clawed up my spine, every instinct screaming:

Run faster.

Branches whipped at my face and snagged my clothes, but I didn't slow down. I pushed myself harder, my legs burning with the effort. My mind was a whirlwind of fear and confusion, the primal instinct to survive overriding all else.

Suddenly, I stumbled into a clearing, the forest opening before me. I skidded to a halt, my breath hitching in my throat. Standing in the middle of the clearing was a massive black wolf, its fur shimmering in the moonlight. Its emerald eyes locked onto mine, glowing with an otherworldly intensity. With a low growl rumbling deep in its chest, the wolf flashed its teeth.

I froze, my heart pounding so loudly I could hear it in my ears. The wolf's gaze was hypnotic, drawing me in even as it terrified me. I took a hesitant step back, my body trembling.

The wolf moved fluidly, almost gracefully, its eyes never leaving mine. It stepped into my path, cutting off any chance of escape. I could see the powerful muscles rippling beneath its fur and the sharpness of its claws as they dug into the ground.

My breath came in short, shallow bursts, fear paralyzing me. I wanted to run, but my legs wouldn't move. The wolf's growl deepened, a sound that seemed to resonate within my very bones. I could feel the primal power radiating from the creature, a force that both awed and frightened me.

Time seemed to stand still as we stared at each other, the forest around us eerily silent. The wolf's eyes seemed to bore into my soul, and for a moment, I felt a strange connection, a sense of recognition. The fear ebbed away, replaced by a curious calm.

Then, the wolf lunged with a suddenness that left me breathless.

I woke with a start, my body drenched in sweat, my heart still racing. The dream lingered, the image of the black wolf with emerald eyes seared into my mind. I could still feel the intensity of its gaze, the primal energy that had coursed through me. With trembling, I embraced my knees to my chest, attempting to dispel the residual fear and confusion.

Looking to my side, the bed was empty, another night alone. The room was bathed in the soft glow of the moonlight streaming through the curtains, which created lengthy shadows on the walls. The silence was deafening, amplifying the loneliness that gnawed at my heart. I ran a hand through my damp hair, the vivid memory of the dream still gripping me.

I swung my legs over the side of the bed and sat there for a moment, staring at the floor. The house was still, except for the faint hum of the refrigerator in the kitchen. I felt a profound sense of isolation, as if the dream had been a vivid illustration of the void in my life.

With a deep breath, I stood up and walked to the window. I pulled the curtains aside and looked out at the moonlit landscape. The world outside seemed so peaceful, a stark contrast to the turmoil within me.

I leaned against the window frame, letting the cool night air wash over me. Maybe the dream was trying to tell me something, a reflection of the inner turmoil I couldn't escape. Perhaps my mind was manipulating me, expressing my deepest fears and desires.

Either way, I knew I couldn't go back to sleep. The restlessness within me was too strong. I needed to clear my head, to find some semblance of peace in the quiet of the night.

So, I grabbed a blanket, wrapped it around my shoulders, and stepped outside into the night, hoping the cool air and the solitude would help me make sense of the chaos within.

As I stepped into the moonlit night, a shiver traced the length of my spine—not from the cold, but from something else. Something unseen. The air, cool and crisp, enveloped me like silk, yet it was the aroma that halted my movement.

Coffee.

The aroma was rich, dark, and warm. The strange aroma clung as if it were a second skin.

I took a deep breath, and the memory of him, his voice, his gaze, and the sensation of his lips on my fingers surged through me.

My muscles loosened before I could stop them, my body responding to the scent like it had been waiting for it all day. It was absurd how quickly the heat stirred in my belly, how my thoughts scattered like leaves in the wind. That smell shouldn't have made me feel this way.

But it did. And for one breathless moment, I wanted to turn back.

I wanted to chase the warmth that was curling low in my core.

"What are you doing outside at this hour?"

The sight of Owen standing at the front door, staring at me strangely, snapped me out of my relaxation. "Don't you have work tomorrow?"

I groaned as the smell vanished and stared hard at him. "Don't you too?"

Before he could answer, I walked briskly past him and returned to the room. It was 3:45 AM.

I tried my best to go back to sleep, but the green eyes from my dream were still there in my mind, haunting me with their intensity, and I was unable to escape the feeling that those eyes were connected to something I couldn't yet understand.

5
THE INTERN

Liliam

I thought I would have a few moments of peace when I arrived early this morning. There's a brief window of time when you can unwind with a cup of coffee before embarking on another demanding day. But halfway through my sip, my phone buzzed with a message from my boss, Mr. Thompson, and I knew those hopes were shattered.

Liliam, please come to my office. I'd like to introduce you to our new intern.

Breathing deeply, I set down the cup and straightened the pencil skirt as I stood up and adjusted the light blue button-down shirt, which I'd tucked inside my skirt to make my outfit as professional as possible. I've tried my best to adjust the tightness of the shirt between my breasts, and I made my way to Mr. Thompson's office. I gently knocked on the door before entering, immediately focusing my gaze on Mr. Thompson's weary face and his salt-and-pepper hair. Thompson seems to constantly comb his slicked-back hair. He was already in his fifties and had a bulgy belly that his belt usually pressed against. He nodded curtly, and his blue eyes gestured to the figure sitting across from him. And my lungs forgot their job.

There he was—the man from the bar. His black hair was well-groomed and slicked back neatly. He looked every bit professional, dressed in a button-up shirt and tie, dark dress pants, and polished shoes. The square glasses perched on his nose gave him an intellectual air, but there was no mistaking those piercing green eyes. Those were the same eyes that had enthralled me earlier that evening.

I tried my best not to stare at how tightly his shirt clung to his chest, stretching over each muscle, outlining the swell of his biceps with sinful precision. My mind betrayed me instantly, conjuring images I had no business entertaining in the middle of the office.

And then there was that smell.

God, the aroma of the coffee cup on my desk didn't stand a chance against this. What lingered on him was richer, darker, and blended with something warm and addictive. It tasted like a blend of coffee and dark chocolate, with a hint of wildness beneath. Earthy. Masculine. Irresistible.

I froze for a second, stunned. He looked up—and I swear the air crackled. His eyes flickered with recognition, but his expression stayed cool and collected.

"Liliam, this is Zeff Gunnolf," Mr. Thompson said, gesturing like this was the most casual introduction in the world. "He's our new intern. Zeff, this is Liliam Black, one of our top employees."

Zeff stood with the kind of ease only someone completely sure of himself possessed. "Nice to meet you,

Liliam," he said, his voice smooth and deep, his hand reaching for mine.

I hesitated—then took it.

His grip was warm, confident, and lingering. The second our skin touched, something sharp and electric zipped up my arm and bloomed under my skin like liquid heat. I bit the inside of my cheek, desperate to keep my voice level. "Nice to meet you, too."

"Liliam," Mr. Thompson continued, "I'd like you to show Zeff around and help him get settled. He'll be shadowing you for the next few weeks."

Of course, he would.

"Of course," I said, smiling through the pulse echoing in my ears. "I'll make sure he gets everything he needs."

We stepped out of the office, and the world outside felt oddly quiet, like someone had muffled the sound. My heels echoed too loudly. His footsteps trailed close behind, steady and deliberate. Too aware. The scent of him swirled around me again—coffee and chocolate, curled low in my belly.

He looked so different in the light. More dangerous. More real.

"So, we meet again," he said quietly.

I glanced at him, pulse racing. "I didn't expect to see you here."

"Neither did I," he replied, and that smirk—God—curved at the corners of his mouth, setting my nerves ablaze. The scent thickened, like he was doing it deliberately, dragging it through the air like a net.

I showed him around, fighting to keep my hands steady and my mind off the image of his mouth on my fingers. But it was hard. Every move, every glance, and every shared breath felt heavy.

When we finally reached my desk, I gestured to the spot beside mine. "This will be your workspace."

He sat, adjusting his glasses with maddening grace. "I'm excited to work with you.

I nodded, my lips parting before I could stop them. "Yeah... same."

As I turned to my screen, attempting to grasp reality, I couldn't shake the feeling deep within me that such an event wasn't a mere coincidence. This was something else. The scent of him, lingering in the air between us, whispered one truth more loudly than anything else: I was already in trouble.

****

The office buzzed louder than usual, the morning air thick with whispers and barely concealed excitement. Coffee cups clinked, keyboards clicked, but none of it masked the true hum of conversation—the new intern.

Zeff Gunnolf.

As I settled into my desk, I could hear the swirl of gossip around me like static.

"Did you see him walk in this morning?" One woman breathed, her voice practically trembling with thirst. "That shirt was painted on."

"And those arms..." another chimed in. "I'd kill to be sandwiched between those muscles."

The words hit like heat. I maintained a fixed gaze on my screen, yet my ears remained unaffected.

"I swear, if he so much as smiles at me, I'm melting."

Someone snorted. "Please, you and every other woman in here."

They weren't even trying to be discreet. Zeff, meanwhile, looked unbothered, sitting calmly at the desk beside mine, shirt sleeves rolled just enough to reveal the dark ink curling around his forearms. His polished shoes were propped casually under the desk, and his posture screamed relaxed dominance. He had that irritating kind of ease. His effortless style drew attention even when he was idle.

"He's working with Liliam, though," someone hissed with thinly veiled disdain.

A pause. Then a collective murmur.

"Of course she gets the hot one," another woman muttered, loud enough for the whole row to hear. "She probably volunteered the second he walked through the door."

"She's always so quiet, but watch—she'll be all over him."

"Do you think she's single?" someone asked.

"No," came a quick answer. "Isn't she with that person? Owen? You know, the moody one on the store floor."

Another voice, sharper now, enters the room. "Doesn't matter. She's got the intern sitting next to her all day. If I were her, I'd be 'training' him all right."

The room echoed with laughter. I felt my cheeks heat, not with embarrassment but irritation. I hadn't done anything—yet suddenly, I was the villain in their fantasies.

The worst part? Zeff hadn't said a word, hadn't even reacted. He just sat there, flipping through a folder like he hadn't just become the center of an office-wide fantasy. And somehow, that worsened it. He knew what he was doing. Every unbothered breath, every flex of his forearm, every subtle glance—it was like he was playing some game I hadn't agreed to join.

And yet, I was already losing. Because it didn't end there.

I'm a woman of responsibility. I work hard, I deliver, and I never slack off. And everyone knew it, which made me the perfect target.

Files began piling up on my desk, one after another, like an avalanche of paper-pushed sabotage. Requests for assistance came in from every direction. Suddenly, I was the goddamn office godmother—fixing broken systems, proofreading sloppy reports, and covering missed deadlines. As usual.

That's the real reason I always ended up training new hires and interns. It wasn't about trust. It was about convenience. What happened this time? It was sabotage dressed as routine.

I recognized it immediately.

They thought if I was busy enough—distracted, swamped—I wouldn't have time to talk to him. They assumed I wouldn't have time to converse with him, let alone breathe around him. They believed that it would be impossible for me to sit too close to him. I unintentionally smiled at him.

"Hey, Liliam, please handle this report for me. I'm swamped," one of them muttered, dropping a thick file on my desk without eye contact.

"Yeah, and I need these sorted out before the day ends," another added, her tone sharp enough to cut glass.

I didn't even bother replying. I just let the weight settle across my shoulders and squared them. *Fine. If they wanted a show, I'd give them one.*

Zeff, meanwhile, was unbothered—focused, calm, and devastating in his quiet way. His rolled sleeves flexed with every keystroke, his jaw tense in concentration. He hadn't noticed the chaos erupting around me, or perhaps he had, but he was allowing me to face my challenges.

I spent the next hour juggling emails, phone calls, broken printers, and three people's worth of work dumped on one desk.

During lunch, I overheard the whispers from the break room. They were louder now. Meaner.

"Did you see how close he sits to her? I bet she loves the attention," one voice sneered.

"She'd better not get too comfortable. Interns don't last long around here," another chimed in, voice like poison dipped in sugar.

I glanced at Zeff's desk—and finally noticed just how dangerously close it was to mine. Barely a breath between them. It appears someone had purposefully blurred the boundaries of professional space.

When our eyes met, a flicker passed between us— unspoken, charged. His smile was small, almost teasing. It sent a pulse of heat straight to my chest.

His presence was a problem. His presence presented a problem that was simultaneously beautiful, maddening, and distracting. I couldn't cease contemplating it. What was the most frustrating aspect? He had no idea of the chaos he caused just by existing across from me.

Just as my patience frayed, a rich aroma hit me—dark roast with something warm and sweet underneath.

I looked up.

A steaming cup of coffee appeared on my desk, Zeff's hand still lightly curled around it. His gaze dipped briefly to my mouth before meeting my eyes.

"Thought you could use a pick-me-up," he murmured, his voice like velvet.

My fingers brushed his as I took the cup, the touch sparking warmth that had nothing to do with the drink. "Thank you," I managed, trying to keep my voice from betraying me.

"Looks like they're piling it on you today," he said, his eyes scanning the chaos of my desk. His tone wasn't casual—it was observant. Protective. Possessive, even.

I gave a breathless laugh. "Yeah. Just a bit."

Then he did something that made my pulse stutter—he reached over and pulled four thick folders off my desk without asking. His hand brushed mine again, intentionally or not, and I nearly forgot how to breathe.

"Zeff—"

"I'm helping," he said firmly. Then, as he leaned closer, he spoke in a softer tone, barely audible above a whisper: "Unless you'd rather I be a distraction instead."

He walked back to his desk, and I couldn't stop my eyes from following him.

The way his broad shoulders moved beneath that crisp button-down—sleeves rolled just enough to show the ink curling up his forearms—was unfair. His pants hugged him perfectly, low on his hips, outlining the powerful build beneath every step he took. Confident. Effortless. It appears he was fully aware of the impact he had.

And God, did he have an effect!

My eyes shamelessly roamed down his back, lingering far too long on the way his shirt stretched across it and how his belt cinched that narrow waist. I bit the inside of my cheek, my thighs pressing together under the desk as heat pooled low in my belly.

Every movement he made felt deliberate, like a slow tease. When he finally sat, legs wide, elbows resting on the armrests, he leaned back with a casual ease that somehow made everything worse.

Zeff didn't even look at me—but I swore he knew I was watching. And maybe he wanted me to.

I dragged my eyes away, forcing myself to focus on the screen in front of me, but my mind was still replaying the shape of his hands, the brush of his fingers, and the low murmur of his voice.

This wasn't going to be easy. He was so close.

Everything about him made my body hum.

I was already familiar with the sensation of his lips grazing my fingers.

****

Zeff

The office was quieting down as the evening wore on. The fluorescent lights cast a stark glow over the nearly deserted room, and the hum of computers was the only sound breaking the silence. I glanced at the clock on my screen: 8:45 PM. Most of the office had already left, but I was still here, determined to make a good impression on my first day.

I looked over at Liliam. She was still at her desk, her eyes drooping, her head slowly tilting to the side. Her hands were resting on the keyboard, but it was evident that she was struggling to fall asleep.

Her exposed neck caught my attention, the soft curve of her skin illuminated by the light from her monitor. My breath hitched, and I felt an intense, primal urge surge through me. Gaius, my wolf, stirred restlessly within me, his instincts screaming to mark her as ours.

"Calm down, Gaius," I mentally whispered, trying to soothe him.

But the sight of her, so vulnerable and unaware, was almost too much to bear. The scent of blackberries filled the air; it was intoxicating, and I had to close my eyes for a moment to regain control.

Slowly, I approached her desk, each step deliberate and quiet. The urge to touch her, to claim her, was overwhelming, but I kept it in check. I reached out and gently tapped her shoulder.

"Liliam," I said softly, trying not to startle her.

She stirred, muttering softly incoherently.

"You are falling asleep," I said with a gentle smile. "It's late. You should head home."

She rubbed her eyes and waved her hand sleepily, as if to dismiss me. "Just a few more minutes…"

But before she could finish her sentence, she leaned down, her head resting on the keyboard. The scene made me chuckle softly. She looked so peaceful, so innocent.

I couldn't resist. My fingers traced the curve of her neck gently, feeling the warmth of her skin beneath my touch. She was tense—overworked and restless. And yet the moment my thumb brushed the spot where her neck met her shoulder, I felt it: the way her muscles softened beneath my hand.

Liliam let out a low, unguarded moan—soft, involuntary, and devastating. It curled around my spine like smoke, pulling something primal loose inside me.

A small smile played on her lips, her eyes fluttering, and I froze for a heartbeat, savoring the sight. The sound of her pleasure—simple, content—was enough to make my pulse falter. I inhaled slowly and deeply, grounding myself before Gaius could rise too close to the surface.

Control. Stay in control.

I let my hand move again, slower this time. More intentional. My thumb swept across the delicate line of her shoulder, kneading the tension out with slow, steady pressure. Her skin was warm. Supple. I could feel her body yielding under my touch; every breath she took was a little deeper than the last.

Her head tilted forward just slightly, giving me more access without a word.

That fact alone aroused me more than I wanted to admit.

It appeared every aspect of her was beckoning me. She shifted slightly and—Goddess help me—leaned back. Against me.

Her head rested dangerously close to my chest, her scent filling every breath I took. I braced my hands on the sides of her chair, caging her in. The soft moan that escaped her lips indicated that she was not merely asleep. It was a reaction. The sound was an echo of the bond we had yet to name.

"Liliam…"

She murmured something incoherent, a mix between my name and a sigh. Her body pressed closer. Warm. Willing. She was unaware of how close she was to unleashing the beast within me.

The sweet tension, as soft as sin, clung to her. My hand moved again, this time sliding down the curve of her neck, slow and firm, feeling how she melted under my touch.

She tilted her head ever so slightly. Her cheek lightly touched my chest. Her slight tilt caused my control to waver.

She doesn't even realize what she's doing to me.

My voice was hoarse when I finally said, "You're falling asleep on me."

"Mmm," she hummed, shifting lazily. "You're warm…"

That did it.

A low growl rumbled from my throat before I could stop it. I stepped back, ignoring the protest of my wolf—and my body, my cock straining with need—as she stirred, her head snapping back slightly from the sound, waking from her sleep.

I'm such a fucking asshole.

She blinked up at me, her lashes fluttering like she hadn't quite surfaced from whatever dream held her. Then she stretched—slowly, lazily, unguardedly. The movement drew my eyes down her frame. The blouse clung to her breasts just enough to spark wild, unwelcome thoughts, and the curve of her hips made something primal twist inside me.

"Let's get you home," I said, my voice lower than I meant it to be. If she gazed at me once more, whispering my name as she had previously, I wouldn't be able to control myself. "And get some rest."

I grounded myself by biting the inside of my cheek.

"Okay, okay," she murmured sleepily.

I helped her gather her things, forcing myself to keep a tight rein on my wolf. I placed a hand gently on her lower back, guiding her toward the elevator. The warmth of her body radiated through my palm. Every step she took beside me felt like a test I wasn't sure I could pass.

As we descended to the ground floor, the soft hum of the elevator surrounded us. Liliam leaned slightly against the wall, her eyes heavy, her body swaying just enough to tempt. The scent of blackberries clung to her like silk—both soothing and torturous.

The doors opened with a quiet ding, and we stepped into the lobby. That's when I saw him.

Owen Greene.

I had been studying Owen Greene for the past 24 hours, following our bar visit. The little information Joah was able to pull didn't say much. Other than that, he served and was discharged months after he met Liliam. They move in together, and ever since, Liliam seems to be the head provider of the stronghold.

That means Liliam worked twice as much as him to provide, and it pissed me off greatly. What kind of man allows that?

He was closing the retail shop in the lobby, but the moment he spotted us, a frown cut across his face like a blade.

"What are you doing here?" He asked, his tone sharp, eyes flicking from her to me like a territorial wolf assessing a threat.

"I was just making sure Liliam got home safely," I said, keeping my tone level but firm. "She was working late."

His eyes narrowed, jealousy flickering just beneath the surface. "And why is that your business?"

Before I could respond, Liliam spoke, her voice soft with sleep. "Zeff works with me, Owen. He's the new intern I'm training."

Owen's expression shifted slightly as he looked at her, but when his gaze returned to me, it was hard and evaluating.

"Alright. Let's get you home then." He stepped forward and took her arm gently, pulling her away from me.

Jealousy surged in my chest like fire, but I forced my face to remain unreadable.

"Thanks for helping her," he said, but his eyes—cold, calculating—told a different story.

"Of course," I replied, meeting Liliam's gaze one last time. "Have a good night."

As they walked away, Owen glanced over his shoulder. His jaw was tight, his stance protective. Possessive. He delivered a menacing gaze without uttering any words.

I clenched my fists at my sides, watching as he placed a hand on the small of her back. My place. My touch. My wolf bared his teeth behind my ribs, snarling low and relentlessly. He doesn't deserve her. He doesn't smell her like I do. Doesn't feel her like I can.

Suddenly, the front door closed behind them, and she vanished from sight.

The lobby felt colder now. Too quiet. My skin prickled with the echo of her warmth. The memory of her leaning back against me, of her body melting under my hand, haunted every nerve. My fingers curled unconsciously, as if still aching for her softness. I could still taste the sleep-heavy sound of her voice when she enjoyed my touch. I still feel the pulse beneath her neck where I'd pressed too close.

And now she was walking away with another man.

I pressed the elevator button harder than necessary and leaned back against the wall, my jaw tight, my eyes burning holes into the empty hallway. That should've been me. Guiding her. Holding her. Tucking her into bed.

Instead, I stood alone in the sterile hum of fluorescent light, left with nothing but the scent of blackberries and the cruel pressure of restraint.

6
TEARS

Zeff

If there was one thing that wasn't different from our world, it was the weight of work. Technology and corporate policies may mask the pace here, but the exhaustion remains the same. It felt the same.

The Pack prioritized community, sustainability, and balance. But here… here you sold your hours to a company. Liliam appeared to dedicate her entire being to this company.

I glanced at the clock on my screen. 1:37 PM.

Liliam hadn't moved from her desk, her shoulders tight and her eyes glued to the monitor. Her fingers flew across the keyboard, her brow furrowed in focused intensity.

"Liliam," I said gently, breaking the quiet hum of her workspace. "Have you eaten anything yet?"

She didn't look up. "Too much to do. I'll grab something later. You should go if you're hungry."

I frowned. This wasn't the first time she brushed off a meal. The dark shadows under her eyes, the stiffness in her posture—she was running on fumes. Gaius stirred uneasily inside me, grumbling his disapproval.

"You can't keep skipping meals," I said, softer than before. "It's not sustainable."

"I'm fine," she replied, her tone tight. "This project is important. I just need to finish—"

I reached out, almost without thinking, and gently took her wrist. Her fingers stilled. The moment our skin touched, something subtle but unmistakable sparked between us.

Warmth.

Her eyes snapped to mine, wide and startled. She pulled her hand away and pressed it against her chest. She looked as if she had sustained a burn.

"You need a break," I said, my tone firmer now, locking eyes with her. "Just a short one."

She opened her mouth to protest, but I wasn't having it. Gaius was already pacing inside me, growling with agitation. Her exhaustion and stubbornness pushed every instinct I had to act. It was my duty to tend to her needs.

Without another word, I reached out and took her wrist again. Her skin was warm—too warm. Like it, remember me. My fingers wrapped around her, and the heat that sparked between us pulsed straight down my spine.

I didn't let go.

"Zeff—"

I ignored the plea in her voice and pulled her gently—but firmly—out of her seat, guiding her toward the elevator. She followed, stumbling half a step behind me.

"What the—"

The elevator doors slid shut behind us, and I pressed the button to the lobby. Her breathing quickened, creating a soft and rapid rhythm that I could sense from her proximity. She hadn't pulled away.

She was still letting me hold her. I kept my hand wrapped around her wrist, trying to ignore how my pulse thudded like a war drum beneath my skin. Her scent—blackberries—wrapped around me like a drug. I could barely focus.

Goddess, why did her touch feel so sinfully erotic?

"We're going to the cafeteria downstairs," I said, my voice rougher than intended. "And I'm buying."

"You don't have to—"

"I insist," I cut in with a smirk. "Boss."

The word tasted dangerous coming out of my mouth, like a dare. Boss me all you want; I'd follow you like a lovesick wolf, panting at your heels and begging to be touched.

She scoffed, but her lips twitched, betraying a smile.

Victory. Small but delicious.

When we reached the café, the warm scents of roasted meats, butter, and fresh herbs drifted through the air. I watched her inhale deeply, and the way her lashes fluttered over her cheek made my gut clench. Her eyes roamed over the glowing food displays with barely contained hunger.

And Goddess, the way her tongue flicked over her lower lip…

I would've dropped to my knees right there.

She moved slowly past the warm bar, her gaze lingering on the roasted chicken glistening beneath the heat lamps and the steamed vegetables glistening with a touch of olive oil. But it wasn't until we passed the cold section that I noticed the true weakness—her eyes landed on the chocolate cake.

It was a massive slice. The chocolate cake was thick, layered, and incredibly decadent.

My mouth curled into a slow grin. Noted.

The dish consisted of roasted chicken, vegetables, and chocolate cake. Unusual. Tempting. Resemble her in every way.

Before she could even open her mouth to place an order, I leaned forward and spoke smoothly to the cashier. "Two plates of roasted chicken and vegetables," I said, then glanced at the dessert display, "and we'll take the chocolate cake."

She blinked, stunned, her brow lifting in quiet surprise. "Observant," she murmured, clearly impressed—though trying to downplay it.

I stepped closer, just enough to feel the heat radiating from her skin. It was magnetic. Irresistible. "Only when it counts," I replied, my voice dropping slightly lower, rougher.

Her breath caught.

And then—just for a second—her eyes flicked to my mouth. Quick. Subtle. But I saw it.

And that was all it took to confirm it.

If I leaned in just a little more… if I whispered her name again, the way I had the night at the office… she might just melt right into me.

With a calmness I didn't quite feel, I led us toward a small table by the window, where golden sunlight spilled across the surface, warming the wood. I pulled the chair out for her, watching how her body moved—smooth and fluid, like temptation wrapped in silk and purpose.

She sat, and I trailed behind, my senses heightened. Goddess, I hadn't even tasted the damn food, and I was already starving—for her.

"You always take care of others," I said as we settled our food. "But who takes care of you?"

She blinked, taken aback by the question. "No one, really. I don't think about it much."

"You should," I said, meaning every word. "You matter too."

She looked away, chewing slowly, and then murmured, "Thank you."

For a while, we ate in silence. Not awkward—just peaceful. Comfortable.

Then, softly, she said, "You're… different."

I tilted my head. "Different how?"

"You notice things," she said, eyes flicking back to mine. "Most people just assume I'm fine. They don't ask. They don't… insist."

"Maybe I'm just stubborn," I said with a small grin. "Or maybe I care."

That made her look down, her lips twitching into a small, unsure smile.

"So," she said, steering the conversation with a sly little smile, "what do you actually like to do—when you're not rescuing exhausted women from screen-induced meltdowns?"

I chuckled, relaxing into the chair. "Touché. I like being outdoors. Hiking, mostly. Nature keeps me sane. It reminds me who I am. Grounds me." I met her eyes with a faint grin. "Also… I read. A lot."

Her eyebrows lifted, clearly intrigued. "What kind of books?"

"Fantasy. Historical fiction. Anything that makes reality feel a little less… ordinary."

"Oof," she said, placing a hand to her chest in mock dramatics. "Same. I grew up obsessed with magic and adventures. Stories were my escape—and my therapy."

I leaned in slightly, lowering my voice. "Do you still read?"

She gave a sheepish shrug. "Not as much as I want to. Life's messy. But I write sometimes... little things."

I raised an eyebrow. "Really? What kind of little things?"

"Short stories. Emotional stuff." She gestured casually, but her eyes conveyed a different message.

"That's amazing." I meant it. "I'd love to read something you've written."

She laughed lightly, her eyes flicking to her cake. "Maybe... someday. If you behave."

God help me. That smile. That tease. I'd behave like hell if it meant reading her words.

We eased into conversation, and it flowed like warm honey. Laughter. Little silences that didn't feel awkward. Her voice became music—low and lyrical, full of color.

Then, I said it.

"I could take you hiking sometime," I offered casually. "Have you ever tried it?"

Her smile slipped just a little, and I caught the tension behind her eyes.

"I... have a partner, Zeff."

I nodded slowly, interpreting her words carefully. "Does he keep you from doing things you enjoy?"

She shook her head. "No. It's just... You're a guy."

I held her gaze, heat simmering low and slow. "I am. And I'm also someone who happens to like talking to you. That's all."

She looked down at the table, hiding a smile. "I'll think about it."

I didn't push. I just watched her, every soft line of her face committing itself to memory.

She picked up her fork and took a bite of the chocolate cake—and instantly her eyes fluttered closed. Her lips parted slightly as she let out the quietest moan of satisfaction.

Fuck.

It looked like she was having a goddamn mouth orgasm.

She chewed slowly, savoring it, and I just stared, completely mesmerized.

"You really like that, huh?" I asked, blinking out of the trance.

"Mmm," she hummed, licking a bit of frosting from the corner of her lips. "This is better than sex."

My jaw clenched. *Wrong. I could do better than that cake any day.*

I grabbed my fork and took a bite.

Too sweet.

I blinked, grimacing slightly. "How can you like that so much? It's like being punched in the tongue by a sugar demon."

She laughed, full and warm. "Because it's decadent and rich and unapologetic. Like all the best things."

I smirked, watching her lick the fork again, and leaned back in my seat, dragging my eyes down her throat as she swallowed.

We should head back, I told myself.

But gods, I wanted to stay in that chair and watch her lick frosting off silver until I lost my mind.

****

A week had passed since I convinced Liliam to take that break for lunch.

Since then, something had shifted—quiet but unmistakable. We worked more easily now. We exchanged subtle glances. We exchanged smiles for a moment longer than necessary. A rhythm had formed between us, easy and unspoken.

But comfort, in an office like this, came at a price.

The moment I stepped in that morning, I felt it. The air buzzed with hushed whispers and tight-lipped smirks. Not the usual office chatter—this was venom disguised as curiosity. The fluorescent-lit corridors pulsated with a current of petty envy.

I didn't need enhanced hearing to catch it. The words hung in the air like smoke—sharp, toxic.

"Did you see how close they were yesterday?"

"She practically melted when he touched her hand."

"She has a boyfriend, right? Owen?"

Owen. The name cut through the noise with a sharp edge. My jaw flexed involuntarily.

I glanced at Liliam. She was at her desk, her face bathed in the glow of her screen, her posture textbook perfect. Too perfect. Her back was too straight, her shoulders too still. She was trying to disappear into the task in front of her—but I knew better. She felt every word.

And they didn't stop there.

"She's got some nerve, acting all innocent."

"Please, if I had a body like that beside me, I'd be wrapped around his desk by now."

"Oh, come on. If I were her, I wouldn't need convincing. Have you seen his arms?"

The laughter that followed wasn't lighthearted. It was mean. Spiteful. Like they wanted her to hear. Like they wanted her to break.

I watched as a folder hit her desk hard.

"Liliam, please handle this for me. It's time-sensitive," one of them said sweetly, though her eyes were ice.

Before Liliam could respond, another one dropped a second stack of files beside it. "And this. Since you're already training the new intern, I figured you'd have time."

I clenched my fists. My wolf, Gaius, growled low inside me.

They're punishing her... for being near us.

She took the papers without complaint. Her jaw tightened, but she didn't say a word. I just added them to the ever-growing pile and continued typing.

But I saw it—her hand trembled for a second before she steadied herself.

What's the most challenging part? No one helped. They watched. Some expressed amusement, while others showed indifference. No one stopped it.

I wanted to stand beside her desk, growl at every one of them, bare my teeth, and demand they show her respect. She didn't deserve this. She was kind. Brilliant. She was far too honorable to respond to the insults they were hurling.

But I knew that wouldn't help the cause.

By lunch, she was unusually quiet. At the café, she picked at her salad, lips pressed together, chewing like it took effort.

"You alright?" I asked gently, leaning in just enough to lower my voice.

She sighed, not looking up. "The whispers are getting old," she muttered, stabbing her lettuce like it had personally betrayed her. "Feels like I'm sixteen again."

"I'm sorry," I said, guilt threading through my chest. "If I'm worsening this—"

"Don't," she said, cutting me off with a worn shake of her head. "You're my apprentice. The spotlight is on them, not you. It's always like this when they don't get what they want."

"There's a reason the company have different employees and their specialties. You are practically running most of the department."

"That's the curse of being talented at what you do," she said with a bitter smile. "They know you'll do a fantastic job. But they'll find ways to isolate you when you don't play along."

I looked down, fists clenched under the table. "They're punishing you… for being decent to me."

She shrugged, but the mask cracked. "It's not just that."

"What then?"

Her gaze met mine. "Look at you, Zeff. You walk in, and the entire room turns into heat and hormones. And they can't stand that you don't look at them—because you're always around me."

The corners of my lips tugged into a smirk. "Is that a problem?"

"It is," she said, and the sharp honesty of it hit like a punch to the gut.

My pulse quickened. "Why?"

"Because you're not Owen." Her voice cracked. Her voice crackled just enough to shatter something within me.

I didn't speak. Just listened. Let her unravel.

She exhaled. "He's been distant for months. I thought it was stress. Or me. That maybe I'd stopped being enough. But the more time I spend with you… The more I start to question everything."

I leaned forward, slowly, my voice quiet but firm. "It's not your fault, Liliam. If he makes you question your worth, that's on him. Not you."

Her eyes shimmered, blinking fast. "You make it sound so easy. But it's not. It's hard to trust again when you give yourself fully… and get burned."

Goddess. My fingers curled under the table. I felt compelled to express my thoughts—yearning to declare that she deserved far more than mere cold hands and insincere affection. Someone like Owen could not possibly understand the depth of what it meant to have her.

But she shook her head, cutting off her pain. "I'm just tired… of holding everything alone."

I didn't hesitate. I moved beside her, slid in close, and wrapped my arm gently around her shoulders. She didn't resist. She leaned in.

But the second her body melted into mine—everything shifted.

Her scent hit me like a drug.

My breath stalled. Sharp. Hot. The subtle sweetness of her warmth, combined with the blackberries in her skin, enveloped me, seeped into my bloodstream, and ignited every cell within me. Gaius stirred. Growled. Low and hungry in the depths of my chest.

Mine.

My nose brushed against her neck before I even realized how close I'd gotten. Her skin radiated heat and pulsed with it. My fingers flexed against her side, desperate for more contact, more anything.

Shit.

Her breath caught.

I felt it—everything.

I could feel the subtle flutter of her pulse beneath my palm. A shiver ran down her spine. The slow, searing wave of heat that rolled off her was not fear. Not discomfort.

Desire.

The desire knocked the breath out of my lungs.

She wanted this.

Her body wanted me.

And that made it so much harder to pull back.

I could taste restraint in my mouth like blood. My hand trembled against her back. My jaw clenched to keep from grazing her throat with my teeth. She was right there—so goddamn close—and I was unraveling.

But I didn't move.

If I ever touched her beyond this point, it would be because she reached out to me.

Even if it burned. Even if my bones yearned for her. Gaius was pacing and snarling, prepared to destroy the world for her.

I pulled away slowly, the heat of her still seared on my skin. My voice was low, rough, and unsteady. "Then let me carry some of it. Even if it's just this moment."

She turned toward me, eyes still wet but unwavering.

And for the first time—she didn't flinch from me.

Her breath brushed my cheek as she whispered, "Okay, just for now."

****

Liliam

I stood by the kitchen counter, a cup of tea in my hand, trying to calm the anxiety that had settled deep in my chest. I had been hoping for a quiet evening, but Owen's footsteps had been loud and heavy the moment he walked through the door.

I braced myself as I heard him pacing from the living room. He had been cold before, but tonight it seemed different, more intense.

"Liliam," his voice came sharp, cutting through the tension in the air, "we need to talk."

I didn't turn to face him immediately, taking a deep breath to steady myself. I knew where the conversation was going. The whispers from the office and the suspicion in his tone had all been building to this moment.

"You've been spending a lot of time with that new intern, have you?" His voice was low, but the anger in it was unmistakable.

My body tensed, and I put the cup down, my fingers lingering over the edge. "What do you mean?"

"I've seen; I've heard things—people at the office talking. They're saying you're always with him. Is that what you've been doing? Are you spending time with him instead of focusing on your life?"

I spun around, hurt flashing across her face. "I'm just doing my job, Owen. Zeff and I have been working on a few things together. It's nothing."

"It's something," Owen snapped. "And I'm not an idiot, Liliam. You think I didn't notice the way you looked at him at the cafe?" His eyes were wild with suspicion now, his hands clenched into fists at his sides. "You think I didn't see the way he looked at you, either?"

My chest tightened. I knew the jealousy had been simmering, but hearing it out in the open stung in a way I hadn't expected. The situation wasn't just about Zeff anymore—it was about Owen's fear, his insecurity creeping in, and his need to accuse me before I could accuse him.

"And what is it that you're so worried about?" I asked, my voice tight, defensive.

Owen's eyes flared, but there was something else there, too—a hint of guilt. "You don't think I know what's been going on? What's been going on between you and him?"

My heart sank. He was projecting his guilt onto me. The guilt he committed years ago—that lie—was a betrayal so deep that it shattered every ounce of trust between us. The pain from that moment was still with me, and now, instead of acknowledging his past mistake, he was accusing me of doing the same thing he did.

"You barely look at me anymore. When did I become a background character in your life?" My voice wavered.

"I walk through the door, you're emotional or withdrawn or—"

"I'm withdrawn because I feel invisible!" My voice cracked.

A beat of silence stretched between us. He looked at me like I was a stranger. It was as if he did not know how we had ended up in this situation.

"I think you've been tense for weeks. And now I walk into a minefield every time I try to talk to you."

"You have not tried, Owen. You barely see me."

He did not reply.

I blinked at him, eyes stinging. "You didn't even notice I cried myself to sleep last week."

His lips parted slightly, like he wanted to defend himself—but nothing came out.

Finally, he exhaled and walked toward the hallway.

"Where are you going?" I asked.

"To pack for my training. My flight leaves at 6 AM. I'll be gone a week."

That was it.

No apology. He didn't fight for anything. Owen flees whenever emotions get in the way.

I stood motionless, my heart thumping—not out of anger, but rather from the oppressive knowledge that I had previously spent months by myself. I was reciting it out loud in my mind for the first time.

****

Zeff

I knew something was wrong.

It sat in my chest like a vise—tight, cold, suffocating. A peculiar, unsettling feeling tugged at the boundaries of my consciousness. It felt like grief. It felt as though I was shedding tears from within. But there were no tears. And that's what unsettled me most.

Such behavior implied that the pain wasn't mine.

It was hers.

The bond was strengthening. The bond was tethering us in ways I hadn't fully grasped yet. And if I could feel Liliam's sorrow bleeding into me... if she had been crying—really crying—then something was deeply, dangerously wrong.

And I couldn't sit still knowing the woman I loved was suffering.

I made my way to the office, heart pounding, hands clenched. I loosened the cuffs of my long blue shirt and rolled the sleeves over my forearms as I entered the building, barely nodding at the receptionist. The cool air within had little effect in relieving the storm gathering in my chest.

I noticed the change in mood right away as I walked to my desk.

Colleagues caught looks, their whispers like invisible knives, sharp and pointed. Their eyes conveyed a clear message, even as their subdued voices faded away like vapor while I walked by.

I later saw her as well.

Liliam came in a little later. Her eyes were red-rimmed and puffy, and her shoulders were stiff. She gave off an empty appearance. fatigued. She appeared as though something within her had taken hold. Her quiet strength, like armor, vanished, replaced by the aching sensitivity of someone who had been carrying too much too long.

She didn't look at anyone. Her head stayed down, her footsteps hurried and unsure. She reached her desk, dropped her bag to the floor with a soft thud, and sank into her chair like gravity had doubled on her.

My hand froze on the headrest of my seat, watching her every movement with razor-sharp focus.

"Liliam," I said, voice low, careful not to spook her. "What happened?"

She glanced up—just briefly—and for a second, I thought she might push me away. But her eyes betrayed her. They shimmered, fragile and raw, and just like that, her composure began to crack.

She turned away, shaking her head, trying to breathe through the storm. I could see the tension in her jaw, the way her fingers trembled ever so slightly as they hovered over her keyboard. I could smell the salt on her skin, the sharp trace of her tears even though they hadn't fallen yet.

It hit me like a blow to the chest.

I moved without thinking.

Reaching for her wrist, I curled my fingers gently around it. Her skin was warm, too warm, and I felt the jolt of her pulse beneath my fingertips.

"Come with me," I murmured.

She didn't protest. Didn't speak. She just let me guide her, her body moving on autopilot as I led her through the maze of cubicles and down a quiet hallway. I opened the door to a smaller, forgotten conference room and pulled her inside, then closed the door behind us with a soft click that seemed to shut out the world.

In the silence, she stood frozen.

Her hands balled into fists at her sides, nails digging into her palms. Her shoulders trembled under the weight of everything she hadn't said. Her breath came in shallow gasps, like she was trying not to break open.

I stood there, helpless, my heart thumping in my throat.

I observed the woman who had once enthralled me, now poised on the brink of a moment she was evidently unable to contain.

Without a second thought, I closed the distance between us in two strides and wrapped her in a firm, unyielding embrace. At first, she tensed, startled—but then she broke. Her body crumpled into mine like a wave collapsing onto shore, and she finally let go. Her face pressed to my chest, her sobs tore through her, raw and uncontrolled, shaking us both.

I held her tighter, her warmth seeping through my shirt, igniting a dangerous ache low in my gut. Her curves and soft breaths perfectly matched my body, as if they were puzzle pieces fitting into place. Her hands clutched at my shirt, desperate, as if I were the only thing anchoring her to the earth.

"I'm sorry," she whispered, broken and breathless, her voice muffled by my chest.

"You don't need to be," I murmured against the crown of her head, my fingers gliding through her hair in a rhythm meant to soothe her—and me. "I've got you."

Her tears soaked into my shirt, each one scalding, marking me. Her pain hummed through our bond like an echo in my bones. I'd never felt so fucking helpless—and never more determined to be the one who improved it.

A small laugh escaped her, cracked and wet, when I asked, "Do you need me to punch him?"

She shook her head, and her hair brushed against my jaw. But then her scent shifted—richer, deeper. Her scent no longer emanated solely from sorrow. Something else. A heady and intoxicating sensation sent a jolt straight down my spine.

Her body trembled, not just from grief... but from something sharper. Her fingers slid down my torso, slow, unsure—curious. And then I felt it: her want. The sensation was hot and quiet, yet it pulsed under her skin like electricity.

My wolf stirred. Gaius let out a low growl in my chest. Mine.

My nose brushed along the crown of her head, drawn by instinct, and I breathed her in—blackberries and the warmth of skin kissed by tension. My hand drifted lower, resting at the small of her back, fingers curling slightly into her, and she shivered under the touch.

"Why do you feel so good?" She whispered, and her voice—goddess-like, thick, breathy, and laced with longing— captivated me. I clenched my jaw, barely keeping myself from answering with my mouth on hers.

"Maybe because you need this," I murmured, my lips grazing the shell of her ear.

She looked up then, her lips parted, her gaze searching mine, as if she already knew we had reached the end of our journey.

Her kiss was hesitant, soft as a sigh—but it shattered me. Electricity exploded across my skin as her mouth met mine. I groaned against her lips, one hand gripping her waist, the other sliding into her hair. She melted into me again, this time not in grief but in need.

I deepened the kiss, tasting and craving her. Her body pressed against mine, hips flush, and when her tongue brushed mine, I lost all pretense of control. My hand found her jaw, tilting her exactly right as I devoured her, desperate to memorize the shape of her mouth.

When I backed her into the door, her breath hitched. She gasped against my lips, her fingers tangling in my hair and pulling me deeper into her heat. My hands roamed—her ribs, her hips, down to the soft swell just above her thigh. She moaned again, and I felt it in my cock, already aching from the weight of this need.

I listened to every sound she released. Her every little sigh had a lasting effect on me. Every whimper. It carved itself into me.

I kissed down her jaw to her neck, biting softly and marking her with my mouth, while she tilted her head and granted me access with a shaky breath.

"Zeff..." she murmured, like a plea and a prayer all at once.

I wanted to answer. I wanted to say everything she needed to hear.

But the moment shattered too fast.

Reality came crashing back. Liliam pushed me aside. I pulled back, my breath ragged, my heart hammering in my chest. Liliam's eyes were wide, her lips swollen from our kiss, and her chest heaving with each breath. I could see the conflict swirling in her eyes—desire, fear, and confusion—all at once.

"I… I can't," she whispered, breaking the silence. "I have a boyfriend."

I froze, every muscle going rigid, my breath still ragged. Her hand rose to her mouth as if she were trying to suppress her emotions again. Hide it. Bury it.

"It's not fair… to him. To you. To me."

I reached for her instinctively, but she took a step back. I should have stopped sooner, should have been stronger, but I couldn't resist her pull, the way her body reacted to mine, or the way her lips felt against mine.

"I… I'm sorry," I whispered, my voice barely more than a breath. "I didn't mean to—"

She took another shaky step back, putting distance between us, her hand covering her mouth as if trying to stifle her emotions.

"I just need time," she said, her voice trembling.

She turned away, her hand still pressed to her mouth, and I watched her go, feeling an ache in my chest. I wanted to reach out, to pull her back, to tell her that everything would be okay, but I knew I had to let her go. She needed to sort through her feelings, and I couldn't force her into anything she wasn't ready for.

When she walked out through that door, leaving me standing there, the realization hit me harder, and I felt more alone than I had in a long time.

The door locked behind her, and I ran a hand through my hair, leaning against the wall. My body continued to tingle from her being against me, and my heart was still racing. Closing my eyes, I inhaled deeply to help me ground myself.

What had I done?

I couldn't help but feel a mix of emotions—regret, longing, and frustration. I desired her more than anything, yet I understood that I could not pressure her nor compel her to make a decision. She had her life, her choices to make, and I had to respect that.

But damn, it was difficult. It was so damn difficult.

7
HIKING

Liliam

I stood at the entrance of the forest trail, arms crossed, my breath catching in the cool morning air. It was Sunday, and after yet another sleepless night, I'd done the one thing I didn't think I would—I'd taken Zeff's advice.

Maybe a hike would help clear my head. Maybe the quiet could untangle the mess inside me.

Maybe I could breathe without seeing his face every time I closed my eyes.

I wasn't the outdoorsy type, and I wasn't dressed for it, but the promise of solitude and fresh air had pulled me out of the house. I needed space, not necessarily from Zeff, but from the shame, guilt, and aching desire I couldn't articulate.

The trail began gently, the trees above forming a leafy canopy that filtered the light into soft golds and greens. I tried to focus on the rhythm of my steps, the steady crunch of gravel and twigs underfoot. But my thoughts kept circling back to that day. My thoughts kept returning to Zeff's arms. His mouth. His voice, rough with need, echoed.

God, what had I done?

Halfway through the trail, the path began to slope unevenly. Tree roots curled over the earth like sleeping snakes, and I, too, lost in my spiraling thoughts, didn't see one until my foot caught on it.

I fell hard.

The ground rushed up, biting at my palms and knees with dirt and sharp gravel. Pain bloomed across my shin as I pushed up with a hiss.

"Great," I muttered, dragging myself upright. "Fantastic idea, Liliam. Real elegant."

I took a shaky step, but my sore ankle buckled slightly on the damp leaves, sending me sprawling again.

"Damn it!" I shouted, slapping the ground, furious at myself. At everything. "Why did I think this was a good idea?"

"Need a hand?"

The voice nearly stopped my heart.

I looked up, startled, breath caught in my throat—and there he was. Zeff

He stood just a few feet away, framed by the filtered sunlight streaming through the trees, his brows slightly drawn with confusion and something softer. Something twisted in my chest. He looked rugged and perfectly at ease in the woods— dark green hoodie clinging to his frame, hiking boots worn in, his stance relaxed but alert, like the forest itself responded to his presence.

But it was his eyes that undid me.

His quiet intensity suggested that he was still thinking about me. It seemed as though he hadn't forgotten about me.

"Zeff?" My voice was barely audible. My heart thudded painfully against my ribs. I never expected to run into any of these people today. "I didn't think I'd see you here."

I hadn't spoken to him since that kiss—since the moment things shifted and spun too fast, too deep. I'd panicked. Vanished. If truth be told, I had ghosted him. It appears I could suppress the lingering energy within me.

I noticed that he had requested Friday and Saturday off, and although I hadn't dared to ask why, a part of me understood that I was the reason.

"I could say the same," he said, his voice low and steady as he stepped closer. "You said you'd think about a hike. I didn't expect you to stumble right into one."

His hand reached out, palm open between us.

I stared at it for a beat too long—then slipped my fingers into his. The moment our skin touched, a jolt ran through me. I could feel the warmth of his touch. It reminded me of the warmth I felt when he held me.

His grip tightened gently, pulling me up with effortless strength. My body rose before my thoughts could catch up.

Standing close enough to feel the warmth radiating off him, I forgot for a moment why I had come here in the first place.

"I wasn't exactly planning to fall on my face," I muttered, brushing dirt off my leggings.

"You're doing fine. Just distracted." He gave me a small, understanding smile. "Mind if I walk with you? I know this trail well."

I almost said no. I almost turned around and ran. But something in his voice—gentle, no pressure—cut through the noise in my head.

I nodded. "Yeah... Sure."

We walked in silence at first. The silence wasn't awkward but rather charged, alive with everything left unsaid.

For days, I'd rehearsed what I would say if I saw him again.

"I'm sorry."

"It was a mistake."

"It can't happen again."

But the truth was, all I could think about was how devastatingly lovely his lips had felt on mine. His hand, strong and certain, had fit against my skin like it belonged there. He seemed to belong there.

Gods, Liliam, the point is to apologize—not fantasize.

And yet, with the trees standing like quiet witnesses around us, the soft crunch of the trail beneath our feet, and Zeff's quiet presence brushing against mine with every step… The words never came.

Because beside him, it didn't feel like an error.

The forest felt different with him in it—warmer, closer. It felt as though the world had released just enough energy to allow us to share this moment together.

I stole a glance at him. His jaw was tight, unreadable. But there was a gentleness in the way his hand occasionally brushed against mine, unintentionally—or maybe not.

The forest seemed less daunting with Zeff by my side, his presence comforting and reassuring. We walked in silence for a while, the sounds of nature around us—the rustling of leaves, the chirping of birds—creating a peaceful backdrop.

I tried to find the words to say anything, but instead I said, "Owen's out of town. Training in the Washington division."

Zeff only nodded. *Yeah, Liliam. It seemed pertinent to the current topic.*

The trail curved upward, and we climbed slowly, the canopy thinning until we reached a clearing. A stretch of valley opened before us—rolling hills and winding rivers blanketed in sunlight. I stopped, awestruck.

"This is one of my favorite spots," Zeff said softly. "It's good for thinking."

I let the silence stretch, the quiet wrapping around us like a soft blanket.

"For what it's worth…" I started to speak but hesitated, saying, "I didn't come out here to find you."

Very stupid, Liliam.

"I know," he said. "But I'm glad I found you."

He turned to face me, his expression serious yet tender. "Come." He offered his hand to guide me down the trail.

I took Zeff's hand, carefully following his lead as we descended along the narrow, winding trail. His steady grip was a constant reassurance, grounding me as we navigated the uneven terrain. The silence between us was comfortable, filled only with the sounds of nature—the rustling of leaves overhead, the chirping of birds hidden among the branches, and the distant murmur of a stream that promised something beautiful ahead.

As we moved deeper into the forest, the sound of water grew louder, the faint murmur becoming a rushing roar. My curiosity was aroused, so I glanced over at Zeff, who smiled knowingly. "You'll see," he said, his voice barely audible over the increasing volume of the running water.

A few moments later, we appeared in a clearing, and I gasped at the sight before us. A magnificent waterfall cascaded down from a cliff above, its waters tumbling into a pool far below. The sunlight filtering through the trees caught in the spray created a shimmering mist that danced in the air. Beyond the pool, a river wound its way through the forest, its waters glittering in the light.

"It's beautiful," I breathed, my eyes wide with awe.

Zeff grinned, pleased by my reaction. "I thought you might like it. Few people know about this spot."

I walked closer to the edge, mesmerized by the sight of the water rushing down. I leaned forward to get a better look at the river below, the roar of the waterfall filling my ears. I felt a sense of exhilaration, a rush of adrenaline at being so close to the edge, to something so wild and untamed.

"Be careful," Zeff warned, stepping closer behind me. "The stones can be slippery here."

"I'm fine," I replied, trying to sound confident even though my heart was pounding. The view from the edge was breathtaking, but I was more focused on not losing my footing. I shifted my weight to get a better look at the waterfall below, but in my haste, my sore ankle betrayed me.

I gasped as my foot slipped, and instinctively, I reached out, trying to grab Zeff's arm. But my fingers barely brushed him as I stumbled forward, the ground beneath me vanishing in an instant.

Panic surged through me as the sensation of weightlessness took over, my stomach lurching as I felt myself falling. My mind raced—this was it. The roar of the waterfall grew louder, the cold mist from the spray hitting my face as I tumbled through the air. Everything was moving too fast, and yet, in that moment, time seemed to slow down. I saw Zeff leap toward me, his eyes narrowed with determination.

We hit the water with a force that knocked the air from my lungs. The icy shock of it stole every thought from my mind as I plunged beneath the surface. The world around me became a blur of bubbles and swirling currents. My limbs flailed in the cold, dark water, disoriented and desperate to find the surface.

For a brief, terrifying moment, I was unsure of which direction to go.

Then, I felt it—a strong hand closing around mine, pulling me up with undeniable force. My chest burned as I fought to reach the surface, and when I finally broke through, I gasped for air, my lungs burning.

Zeff was beside me, his grip firm, his presence an anchor in the chaotic waters. "I've got you," he said, his voice calm but strained. His hair was slicked wet to his forehead, and the intensity in his eyes told me he was just as shaken as I was, though he masked it well.

"You okay?" he shouted over the roar of the waterfall.

I nodded, still catching my breath, the adrenaline coursing through my veins. "Yeah… I think so."

Zeff's expression softened with relief, and he gave me a small, reassuring smile. "Hold on to me," he said, wrapping an arm around my waist to keep me close. Together, we swam away from the base of the waterfall, the current pushing us downstream.

The cold water rushed past us, but Zeff's strong arm around me was a steady anchor. He guided us toward a calmer part of the river, where the current was gentler, and we could find our footing. I could feel the strength of his body beside mine, the warmth of his skin even in the chilly water.

When we finally reached the riverbank, Zeff helped me up onto the rocky shore. I sat down, still catching my breath, my heart pounding in my chest. The rush of the fall, the shock of the cold water, and the exhilaration of being so close to Zeff overwhelmed me.

Zeff knelt beside me, his eyes filled with concern. "Are you sure you're okay?"

I nodded, a shaky laugh escaping my lips. "Yeah, I'm… I'm okay. That was… unexpected."

He chuckled, a hint of relief in his eyes. "You sure know how to make a hike interesting."

I laughed again, the tension easing from my body. "I guess I do."

I'd spent the past few days running from him—from the kiss, from the feelings I would rather not name. But now, soaked and shivering, with his arm wrapped tightly around me and his scent tangled in the air between us, I couldn't lie to myself anymore.

Part of me needed him.

That part of me blindly trusted him. That part of this man has ignited something so deep and dark in me I didn't know I had. Every time he touches me, the coiling heat of desire only intensifies.

He looked down at me, water dripping from the sharp line of his jaw, his green eyes locked on mine with a heat that burned through the cold. His chest rose and fell with restrained tension, his hand still gripping my waist like he was afraid I'd disappear.

"Still think coming out here was a bad idea?" He asked, his voice low—half-teasing, half-serious.

I didn't answer right away.

In that instant, nothing about this felt like a mistake.

My gaze swept over him, his soaked shirt clinging to hard muscle, the storm's shadows making him appear carved from the night itself. And when I looked back into his face, I let my gaze say what I couldn't yet voice aloud.

This new part of me screamed, "I wanted him."

Completely.

Utterly.

His jaw tensed, like he felt it—the shift in me. His gaze dropped briefly to my mouth, and I didn't move. Didn't flinch. I just watched him.

Come closer.

Touch me again.

Take what we both know is yours.

He swallowed hard. I caught the flicker in his eyes—the war between control and the pull clawing beneath his skin. The same pull is ravaging mine.

I've always drowned myself in corny fantasy books when reality feels like a dull blade scraping bone. Soulmates. Magic bonds. I experienced fated touches and forbidden kisses. That was my escape. I used it as a coping mechanism when life seemed bleak and the longing for something more became too intense to ignore.

If I couldn't live it, at least I could read it. Dream it. Pretend.

But here, in this storm-lit silence, everything logical inside me lit up like a crashing plane's dashboard—warning lights blinking in wild distress. And I wasn't crashing into reality.

I was plummeting into fantasy.

Into him.

My body spoke a language my mouth hadn't yet dared whisper. Needed to radiate off my skin. Desire curled around my spine and pressed heat between my thighs.

****

Zeff

She looked at me.

No—she was checking me out.

She didn't look at me in a polite, casual manner. No, Liliam looked at me like she was searching for something in the ridges of my face, something hidden behind the storm-soaked skin and the careful calm I wore like armor.

Her gaze dragged over me slowly—deliberately—and I felt it like a touch. Her gaze dipped to my chest, where my soaked shirt clung like a second skin, outlining every breath. The way her eyes lingered on my throat, then on my lips, was captivating. It appears she could still detect my taste.

It wasn't shy.

It was heat—buried beneath hesitation and fear, but unmistakable. A silent confession.

And Goddess, help me, it nearly undid me.

I felt my muscles coil, tight with restraint. My jaw ached from holding back the groan threatening to rip from my throat. Gaius surged forward within me, his claws scraping against my ribs, urging me to act—close the distance, pull her against me, and savor her once more until she forgot every reason we should not engage in this.

But I held still.

Barely.

Her eyes finally met mine, and I saw it. The storm is behind them. It was more than just fear; it was deep and intense desire. The desire was raw, wild, and on the brink of unraveling.

And suddenly the world around us disappeared. The forest. The storm. She found herself cut off from everything else.

She was trembling. She was trembling not only due to the cold but also due to the adrenaline still coursing through her system. I could hear it in the rhythm of her breath, the way it hitched. I could see it in the way her fingers clutched the edge of her wet sleeves, knuckles white, and shoulders tight with tension. Her clothes clung to her like a second skin, and her lips—already turning blue—made something deep in my chest twist.

I shook the water from my hair, flinging droplets into the air, and motioned to the trail.

"Come on," I said, gentler than I meant to. "You're shaking like a leaf. Let's get you somewhere warm."

She didn't argue.

The walk was quiet, our soaked clothes squishing softly with every step. Leaves clung to her legs, and her shallow breaths fogged faintly in the cool air. But at every pace, the sound of raindrops intensified, and I knew we had to hurry. Every few paces, she glanced at me—like she wasn't sure if I'd vanish again the moment she blinked.

She acted as if we hadn't shared a kiss. Like she hadn't run. Like I hadn't let her.

The tension between us was thick—humid, electric, soaked in everything we hadn't said. But I didn't push. Her appearance left me speechless. She was fragile, haunted, and gorgeous. My wolf was pacing just beneath my skin, wild with the urge to claim her.

We reached the cottage. The cottage was a solitary room, partially buried in the hill and engulfed by moss and stone. When the world became too noisy, I found refuge in this place. Dry. Warm. Ours.

"This is where I used to come when I needed space," I said, unlocking the door. "When things get… complicated."

Yes. When my body usually feels like it's on fire and I want to fuck the living thing out of someone.

She stepped inside slowly, her gaze sweeping the cabin like she was walking into something intimate. The faint scent of pine and smoke lingered, clinging to the wooden walls like memory.

"You've spent nights here?" She asked, her voice soft, a little breathy.

"Days," I said, crouching by the fireplace. "Sometimes weeks. It's easier to breathe here."

She nodded faintly but didn't move further. Her arms were wrapped tight around herself, her silhouette haloed by the firelight I sparked to life.

Goddess, Parr Season will be tortured here with her smell lingering.

"You need to get out of those wet clothes before you freeze," I said gently, glancing over my shoulder. "You'll catch something."

"I don't have anything to wear."

I turned somewhat too slowly. She had already started to flush. from the cold. from nerves. From me?

My fingers brushed the familiar folds of wool as I rummaged through the ancient cedar chest. I took out my thickest blanket, which smelled of pine smoke and cold evenings and was rough and earthy.

It smelled like me.

Soon, it would smell like her.

I held it out. "Here. Use this."

"Thanks," she whispered, her voice soft—unsure. Her fingers grazed mine as she took it, just a whisper of contact, but it struck me like a brand.

The heat surged through my hand, up my arm, and directly into my core. I turned back to the fire, clenching my jaw. I needed something to focus on—anything that wasn't the image of her holding that blanket against bare skin.

And then I heard it.

I heard a gentle rustle.

The wet sound of fabric peeling from skin was audible.

The wooden floor echoed with the weighty fall of clothes.

My spine went rigid.

She was undressing. She was just a few feet behind me. She was fully nude beneath the blanket. Wrapped in my scent.

I gripped the fire poker tighter, the iron groaning beneath my fingers. My breathing slowed, deeper and heavier. Her scent drifted to me—warm now, tinged with skin and heat and something unmistakably hers. It filled my lungs like a drug, flooding my veins with fire.

Gaius stirred violently, his growls thick and feral. **She's right there. Take her. Claim her.**

No. Not unless she asks for it.

But Goddess, my mind had already let me down—already pictured the gentle curve of her hips, the way her back arched as she moved under that wool. I could feel a tightness building up inside my jeans, a familiar ache that reminded me of my younger days when all I wanted was to find some kind of release.

She was so close. I could hear the shift of her body on the bed and feel the ripple of her breath across the room. The firelight painted the walls in soft golds and shadows, and all I could think about was what her silhouette would look like bathed in that light—bare, flushed, stretched across those blankets.

My throat burned as I swallowed back the growl rising in my chest.

Focus. Control.

However, the air between us now carried a charge, static and smoldering. Even a whisper of my name would send me reeling.

I closed my eyes, willing my hands to steady. Restraining the beast within me was not as difficult as preventing her from witnessing my intense desire to surrender to it.

"How about you?" She inquired from behind me, her voice barely audible over a whisper.

I stood and peeled off my hoodie. The fabric dragged against my skin, dripping. Her breath caught.

I didn't look. But I felt her eyes. I felt the heat of them crawling over my back like fingertips.

"I know how to survive like this," I said, my voice rougher than I intended. "Fire. Shelter. Vodka usually solves the problem."

My jeans clung to my skin—heavy, soaked, and cold. Every shift, every movement, reminded me how tightly they wrapped around me, how painfully aware I was of her presence. I stole a glance behind me.

She was standing by the bed, wrapped in my blanket, the thick wool falling to her knees. Damp strands of her dark hair clung to her neck and collarbone, and her skin, flushed from the cold—or maybe something else—glowed in the firelight.

But her eyes...

Her gaze fixed itself on my stomach.

She focused specifically on the area just above my navel, where my fingers had started undoing the button of my jeans.

Her throat bobbed in a nervous swallow, and I froze.

"May I?" I asked, my voice quiet now. Controlled. But there was no hiding the tension beneath it—the heat that pulsed through me.

She startled, color blooming across her cheeks as she quickly turned her face away, staring hard at the wall like it held the secrets of the universe.

"Go ahead," she murmured, barely above a whisper.

I didn't let myself linger. I turned back to the fire and pushed the jeans down, slowly, carefully. The fabric dragged over skin—tight over the rigid strain in my boxers. Every movement was deliberate, almost punishing. My cock was hard—aching from the friction and the restraint—and now barely contained beneath thin, soaked cotton.

Goddess.

I placed the wet jeans near the fire to dry, careful not to look at her again. If I did, I wasn't sure what would happen.

Instead, I sat down, my back pressed to the edge of the bed, legs bent, and arms resting across my knees. The fire cracked and popped softly in front of me, its warmth licking across my skin.

I was close enough to feel the heat.

I remained at a safe distance to maintain control.

I could hear her adjusting and cuddling further into the wool behind me, as well as the gentle rustle of the blanket. The distance between us hummed with tension, need, and something neither of us dared to define yet.

I didn't turn around. But I felt her gaze on me. Like a touch I hadn't earned—yet.

What's the most challenging aspect? I would rather not earn it with patience.

I wanted to take it. Every inch of her.

But instead, I breathed slowly. I maintained my focus on the fire.

Let the ache simmer.

I assured myself that I could endure this. Even as my body screamed otherwise.

Her movements shifted on the bed—quiet, soft, and intimate in their simplicity. I didn't have to look to know she was settling against the blanket, but I did anyway.

Slowly. Purposefully.

Her shoulder had slipped free, exposing flushed skin kissed by firelight. The line of her collarbone, the tender curve of her neck—it hit me like a punch to the gut. I couldn't tear my eyes away.

"I'm such a mess," she murmured, eyes cast down. "You wouldn't be drenched if it weren't for me."

"Best mess I've gotten into in a while," I said, my voice husky with more meaning than I should have let slip.

Her lips curled, trying to suppress the smile, but it broke through anyway—a soft flicker of light in her storm. Something vulnerable. Beautiful.

I rose, crossed the cabin, and grabbed the vodka from the cabinet, offering it to her without a word. Her fingers brushed mine again, intentionally this time. Her touch lingered longer than necessary.

She took a sip and winced, coughing softly. "Strong."

"Yeah," I smirked. "It burns the bullshit out."

Her laugh was quiet, a breath of something warmer, but the fragility in her posture was still there. Her shoulders were tense, her body coiled like a wire under silk. The blanket dipped lower as she shifted, revealing a stretch of thigh that made my chest seize.

Bare. Smooth. The fire's amber glow illuminated the scene like a painting.

Fuck.

I sat down on the floor beside the bed again, pretending to reach for the bottle—anything to keep from staring. I took a slow drink and almost groaned. Her lips had touched the rim. Her taste mingled with the vodka.

Best goddamn vodka I've ever had.

Then—her hand.

Fingers slid into my damp hair, hesitant but electric. They skimmed through it slowly, like she was testing what I'd do. What I'd allow. My entire body stilled as my skin erupted in goosebumps. A twitch shot through my cock. I clenched my teeth.

"Zeff…" she breathed.

Her voice, shaped around my name, undid me.

I turned, met her eyes—and time stopped.

There it was.

It was more than just an attraction. It was more than just a sensation of warmth. The need.

The need to be seen. To be touched without judgment. To be safe. To be wanted for more than what she was running from.

Her eyes pleaded, *"Can I trust you not to break me if I give you everything?"*

But I could also see the fear. That fear of the unknown. Humans often experience this common fear, which obscures their instincts.

"What is it?" I asked, my voice rough and unsteady.

She hesitated, her lip trembling. "Nothing," she whispered. "Just… thank you. For being here."

The crack in her voice sliced through every defense I had.

I leaned in, the fire's warmth kissing my bare chest. My voice dropped to a rasp. "You don't make things harder, Liliam. You're not a burden. I'm here because I want to be."

She didn't blink. Didn't breathe. Just watch me.

I could've kissed her. Should have.

But she had to be the one to reach out first—when she was ready. When her fear no longer outweighed her desire, I promised myself not to be like the rest. I want her to choose me. She chooses to be with me because she desires it.

"Just rest," I murmured. "You're safe here."

She nodded, burrowing deeper into the blanket. But her eyes stayed locked on mine, as if afraid I might disappear the moment she closed them.

I turned back to the fire, hands reaching for the poker to stoke the embers, but my body was still on edge—every nerve strung tight.

The scent of her wrapped around me like a drug.

The rain outside eased into a whisper.

But inside this cabin, inside me—the storm was only beginning.

She didn't know it yet.

But she was burning too.

****

I felt a warm presence.

As a werewolf, I find it unnatural to feel such things. We are warm by nature. What could possibly be this warm?

It was soft, pulsing, and inviting—drawing me from sleep like a tide dragging me toward shore. My mind was fogged, heavy, and suspended somewhere between a dream and waking.

The fire was still glowing. The scent of damp pine and smoke lingered in the air.

My eyes focused on the cabin.

And then I saw her.

She stood near the fireplace, completely bare, glowing in the firelight like she belonged to another world. Her hair cascaded down her back in loose, damp waves, her skin glistening in the amber light, her curves dipped in shadow. My mouth went dry.

I blinked once. Twice.

My hand reached across the sheets. Wait—when did I got into the bed? All I remember was drinking the vodka bottle and… Instinctively, my hand reached out—searching for something I already knew was missing. The bed was warm but empty beside me.

Where she should've been, there was only the ghost of her heat. Her body left a hollow curve in the mattress.

"Liliam—?"

I meant it to sound like a command. A warning. Perhaps it was even a plea.

But it came out broken—nothing more than a whisper laced in gravel and ache.

And then she turned.

She stood at the hearth, her bare skin painted in firelight.

She wasn't just beautiful. She was devastating. She was a vision of soft destruction.

Her hair, unbound, spilled down her back in dark, silken waves. The flicker of flame kissed her every curve—the elegant slope of her spine, the arch of her hips, and the fullness of her thighs. Her skin glowed like sun-warmed ivory, and the delicate peaks of her breasts stood taut in the heat, begging for touch.

And between her legs—gods, I nearly lost myself. The soft, inviting warmth of her womanhood glistened like temptation incarnate.

Her amber eyes met mine, and everything stilled. Time, breath, thought.

She didn't speak. She didn't need to.

Desire dripped from her gaze like honey, slow and heavy. It shimmered around her like heat rising off desert stone—intangible yet suffocating in its intensity.

My lungs forgot how to work.

But my cock didn't.

No, the traitor surged with life—rising, hardening, responding to her like a flower blooming toward the morning sun.

Need coiled inside me like a beast stirring from slumber. My whole body lit up; every nerve was aware of her. Only her.

She strode towards me with purpose, and when her finger pressed softly to my lips, my body roared in response.

Everything inside me—human and wolf—snapped to attention. My blood surged. My cock throbbed painfully beneath the blanket as she climbed onto my lap, skin brushing skin, her body so warm, so alive, so real. The aroma of her, a blend of blackberries and weed, enveloped me intensely. I nearly came undone right there. My thoughts—what little remained—crumbled under the weight of her.

"Is this real?" I meant to ask, but it never made it past my throat.

Her hands traced down my arms—feather-light and deliberate. My muscles flexed beneath her touch, instinct overriding thought. A growl built in my chest, low and primal, vibrating through my ribs as her scent wrapped around me like smoke.

Gaius growled. Possessive. Wild. Insistent.

She settled on top of me, every inch of her pressed against my chest, her legs straddling my hips. The pressure and friction ignited a spark that had been simmering since our first encounter.

Her lips hovered above mine, her breath soft and shallow.

Then she moved. Her hips rolled forward, slow and deliberate, dragging a tortured groan from my throat. My hands rose on instinct, gripping her thighs and her waist. I needed to feel her, grounding myself in her.

"Liliam," I gasped again, but she silenced me with a kiss—deep and claiming.

I opened to her like a starved man, kissing her back with everything I had. Our mouths moved in perfect sync, teeth clashing, tongues tangling. I bit her lower lip, and she gasped—gods, that sound—and I nearly lost it.

She arched into me, her nipples brushing my chest, and I bucked beneath her, helpless to stop the way my body responded. My hands slid up her back, down her ass, squeezing, guiding her rhythm. She moaned, the sound vibrating through me like a command.

Every instinct screamed, "Take her." Mark her. Claim her. Now.

She whispered my name again, breathless, almost reverent, and that was it—I gave in.

I flipped us in one fluid motion, laying her down on the blankets, covering her with my body. My mouth found her throat, trailing kisses along her collarbone, down between her breasts. Her hands tangled in my hair, pulling me closer, deeper, her back arching, thighs parting beneath me.

When I finally slid into her, she cried out—a broken, beautiful sound that shattered the last piece of my restraint.

We moved in unison, as if destined for this moment. Her body fit mine perfectly, hips rising to meet every thrust, nails digging into my back, dragging me closer, anchoring me in the fire of her.

Her skin burned against mine, slick with heat and want, and my wolf howled—mine, mine, mine. Every movement was desperate, sacred, and frantic with the need to merge, to become.

She whispered something—my name, a plea, a curse, maybe all three—and her body clenched around me as she came, her legs locking around my waist, pulling me closer to her.

And just as my need exploded—just as I let go—

I gasped awake.

My back hit the wall behind me, breath catching like I'd been punched in the chest. My hands—half transformed into claws. My teeth elongated and sharpened. My muscles locked in place as the burn of shifting surged through me.

Gaius was right there, clawing beneath my skin.

"Damn it," I growled, pressing the heel of my hand to my temple.

The room was still dark, save for the dying embers of the fire. Liliam lay curled on the bed, her breathing soft and even, the blanket half-slipped from her shoulder.

Peaceful. Unaware. Untouched.

I stood slowly, every part of me trembling from the strain of holding back. My blood still boiled, my cock hard and aching with a need I hadn't had the chance to release. My wolf growled, insisting that I complete the task the dream had started.

But I wouldn't. Because she wasn't ready. And that meant we weren't.

I stumbled to the door, barefoot and bare-chested, forcing myself outside into the cool night air. The forest swallowed me in silence. The sky was thick with clouds, the moon hidden, and the trees tall and shadowed.

My breathing was ragged, my chest tight. My wolf was seconds from taking over.

So, I let go.

Pain tore through me as bones cracked and shifted, fur bursting through skin. Gaius took over with a triumphant roar, and we ran—wild and reckless. Through trees. Over rocks. Running into the wind is a common experience.

Running to forget the taste of her skin in my mouth.

I was running because it was the only thing standing between me and disaster.

Running to remember that I loved her enough not to touch her until she asked me to.

8
SHADOW

Liliam

I woke with a gasp, heat pooling low in my belly. Zeff's hands. He planted a kiss on my neck with his lips. In the pit of my throat, his voice growled my name. His warm body weighed heavily on me. The sensation of him entering and exiting my body penetrates me profoundly.

I've never felt anything like it. Hell, I've never dreamt anything like this. It had felt so real—so visceral, so consuming—that my whole body trembled with the ghost of it.

My heart thundered as I sat up in the dark. The fire had long since died down, leaving only faint embers flickering in the hearth. The blanket had slipped halfway off my body, my bare legs tangled in the sheets, my chest rising and falling too fast.

I looked over beside the bed at the spot I saw Zeff last night, drinking. And it was empty.

The dream had already made me breathless, but the cold silence that followed twisted something sharp in my chest.

"Zeff?" I whispered, my voice rough.

No answer. Only the distant rustle of the forest beyond the walls.

I swung my legs off the bed and rubbed my face, trying to make sense of everything. My skin still buzzed from the way his dream-self had touched me, kissed me, and filled me. God, I could still feel the weight of him between my thighs.

What the hell was happening to me?

I spotted a dark flannel shirt near the nightstand—his, no doubt. Desperate for something to feel anchored, I pulled it over my head. It hung loose on my frame, swallowing me whole, but it smelled like him. Warm skin. So, him. I closed my eyes and inhaled, trying to steady the fire still smoldering inside me.

I grabbed my underwear, still a bit damp but wearable, and slid it on. The rest of my clothes were useless. As I stood, the faint howl of a wolf echoed through the trees outside, long and mournful.

My pulse spiked.

"Zeff?" I called again, louder this time, but the only reply was the wind and the distant, answering howls.

Where the hell was he?

Panic clawed up my throat. I scanned the room for something—anything—I could use, and my eyes landed on a thin iron poke near the fireplace. It wasn't a weapon, but it was powerful enough to do anything my hands wouldn't.

I stepped toward the door, gripping the iron poker with both hands. The moment I opened it, the forest air rushed in, cold and biting against my bare legs.

The night was black—pitch, starless. The trees were silhouettes in the dark, and every sound around me was magnified: twigs cracking, leaves whispering, and a low growl somewhere far but not far enough.

I moved forward, feet crunching softly over the forest floor, each step unsure.

The dream clung to me—every kiss, every moan. I felt him on me, inside me, and it blurred with the worry blooming in my chest.

"Come on, Liliam," I muttered, forcing myself to keep walking. "Don't be a coward. Just find him."

A sudden rustling to my left made me jolt. I spun instinctively, yelping as I swung the iron poke with all the force adrenaline could summon.

Swoosh—

Zeff dodged—barely—his head jerking back just as the poker sliced through the space where his skull had been.

"Hey!" He barked, half-crouched, one hand up in defense, the other gripping a bundle of clothes. "It's me!"

The iron dropped from my hands with a heavy thud, hitting the mud like it had scorched my palms.

My breath came hard, chest heaving.

"Damn," he muttered, standing upright, brushing the hair from his face. "At least I know you can swing like a pro ballplayer."

"Zeff!" I hissed, storming over to him, heart pounding from the scare. My palm smacked hard against his bicep—not once, but twice.

He flinched, but only slightly, more amused than frustrated. "Ow," he said with a grin, eyes glinting. "Okay, I deserved that."

And that's when I noticed.

He was shirtless. His skin glistened with rain, water tracking down the ridges of his chest. And he wasn't wearing anything underneath those jeans—nothing. The denim hung low, teasing the sharp V-line that led down to—

My gaze shot back up to his.

His jaw flexed. Tightened.

His green eyes darkened—black flashing through them like lightning through a storm cloud.

"You're wearing my shirt," he said, voice low.

I swallowed. "It was the only dry thing."

The air shifted. The tension was so intense that even a blade could sever it.

"You needed dry clothes," he murmured, his voice suddenly quieter, rougher. His eyes moved over me, slow and reverent—his flannel swallowing my frame, my bare legs exposed, my fingers still trembling from the rush.

And for one long second, neither of us moved.

And my heart hadn't stopped hammering—not from fear, but from him.

He reached out, his hands finding my shoulders, steadying me. His touch—warm, solid—eased something in me. And at the same time, it reignited everything I'd tried to bury.

His body was still damp from sweat. His chest rose and fell with controlled breaths, but I could feel the heat rolling off him. Too close. Too tempting.

I glanced away, the scent of his skin and the memory of that dream overwhelming me. I wanted to lean in to see if it would feel the same. But I held myself back.

A faint, high-pitched whimper, fractured and shivering, echoed through the trees. It was barely more than a breeze, but it snapped the silence like a string pulled too tight.

Zeff stiffened beside me. His entire frame tensed; eyes narrowed as he scanned the darkened canopy. I held my breath.

There it was again. Closer now. The sound was a soft, broken cry, thin and breathy, like a child muffling their sobs in the dark.

"What's that?" I whispered, barely audible.

But something more than curiosity tugged at me. It was not only a sound or plain concern but a force that was deeply rooted in my nature. There was a force equivalent to gravity beneath my ribs, urging me to walk forward. Calling.

Zeff's hand shot out instinctively to stop me, fingers brushing my arm—but I moved. It felt like a call to action. My body refused his caution.

The sound came again. Urgent now. Like a wounded thing begging not to be left behind.

I moved faster, my feet brushing wet leaves, dodging low branches, and stepping over roots like I had walked this path in dreams. I couldn't explain it, but I felt drawn—as if the forest itself was parting just for me.

Then I saw it.

A flicker of dark gray fur appeared beneath the thicket. Small. Still. Trembling.

I froze.

Curled against the gnarled roots of an old tree was a pup, soaked, shivering, ribs showing through thin, matted fur. His small frame was tucked tightly into himself, like he was trying to disappear.

My heart shattered open.

But before I could take a step, a low, guttural growl vibrated through the underbrush.

I turned slowly.

A larger gray wolf stood just beyond the trees—fangs bared, hackles raised. Its eyes locked onto mine, wild and burning. I must have stepped between the line of sight of the gray wolf and the pup.

Zeff's voice came low and fierce through the trees. "Don't move."

The wolf growled deeper, taking a step forward. Its body was coiled like a spring, ready to lunge.

I didn't think. I acted on instinct—and maybe a little stupidity.

I stomped hard on the ground and flung out my arms like I was shooing away a stray cat.

"Go!" I shouted. "Go away!"

The wolf stopped. Its ears twitched, and for a moment—just one heartbeat—it stared at me. Something passed behind those eyes… not anger. But recognition.

Then, with one final growl, it backed into the trees and vanished like smoke.

I exhaled in a rush, my whole body trembling. The tension drained from me in one sweep.

I turned back to the pup. He hadn't moved, but his golden eyes were watching me now—uncertain, wary.

I knelt, slow and deliberate, careful not to startle him. "Hey there," I murmured, my throat tightening. "It's okay. I'm not going to hurt you."

He whimpered—low, unsure—and let out a growl that was more instinct than threat. A warning wrapped in fear.

"I know," I said softly, extending my hand palm-up. "You're scared. But you don't have to be."

Behind me, I heard the snap of a twig.

Zeff knelt at my side without a word, the heat of his presence grounding me instantly. The pup looked between us. He let out another, softer whimper. He sniffed the air. No growl.

Zeff leaned in closer, his voice a warm rumble. "It's okay, little guy. We've got you."

The pup sniffed the air again, then—tentatively—took a step forward. His nose brushed against my fingers, and I felt something electric pass between us.

A Connection.

The pup's golden eyes stared into mine. And in that moment—everything else vanished.

The forest faded. The breeze stilled. My breath felt... borrowed.

There was no logic behind the feeling. No reason. There was an eerie, quiet tug, akin to gravity reshaping the world until we were the sole entities remaining. My fingers trembled as I reached out—not out of fear, but something far stranger.

A low, desperate whimper left him. Then he moved—crawled the last inch between us—and touched his forehead to my palm.

And there was this tingling feeling; something inside me shifted. A spark. A thread tightening. I sensed a feeling beyond my own, yet I managed to comprehend it.

The pup pressed against my hand again, then let out a small sigh. His body leaned into me and curled close to my knees.

Zeff exhaled behind me, low and quiet. I turned slightly, expecting him to speak—but he didn't right away. He just stared. His eyes had changed—widened, like he was thinking but couldn't figure it out.

"What... just happened?" I whispered, still stroking the pup's trembling back.

Zeff blinked, then gave a small, almost forced smile. "He's just... trusting you," he said carefully. "He must sense that you're not a threat."

"That's more than trust," I murmured.

Zeff nodded, his smile tight. "Maybe he feels safe with you."

The words were gentle. Easy. But something in his voice told me he didn't believe it was that simple.

He was trying to avoid making a big deal out of it.

I looked back down at the pup. His breathing had slowed. He pressed his body into mine, as if I was already his home.

"I felt something," I whispered. "I don't know what it was, but when I touched him… it was like something inside me answered."

Zeff didn't respond at first. His eyes flicked between me and the pup, then at the forest.

"He's just scared," I said quietly, carefully. "You're calm. He feels that."

But it didn't feel like that.

It felt like he'd recognized something in me that I didn't even know I had.

Still, I didn't push. Instead, I pulled the pup closer. His body shivered once, then melted against my arms like he'd been waiting for this.

For me.

Zeff sat beside me silently, close enough to feel, far enough to give space. And when I glanced sideways at him, his eyes weren't on the pup anymore.

They were on me.

He was watching me as if he had seen a door open within me and was uncertain about what might emerge.

****

Zeff

I'd seen a lot in my life.

I had witnessed the ferocious fury of wild wolves. I had witnessed pack challenges that ended in blood and broken bones. I'd stood witness to the sacred rites of ascension, to alpha lines being claimed in howls and agony. I'd seen pups born slick with blood and instinct, watched territories carved with claws and will.

But nothing—nothing—had prepared me for this.

The moment my eyes locked with the gray wolf's, I let the dominance rise. Not loud. Not threatening. Just… present.

There was a force that pulsed through my bones, communicating in the age-old language of posture and gaze. It wasn't a fight. It didn't need to be.

The wolf recognized it.

An Alpha.

The beast held my gaze for a heartbeat longer—defiant, not submissive. However, it didn't act foolishly. There was a flicker of something else in its eyes before it backed away. Respect? Resignation?

Then it turned, melting into the forest with the silence only wild things carry.

The world possessed a harsh sense of humor. The longer you gazed at it, the deeper its sarcastic streak became. I believed it was fate when I witnessed Liliam kneeling in the dirt, her hair shimmering in the silver moonlight, and her shoulders tensely reaching out to a solitary pup. Just the bond.

The pup didn't merely approach her. He chose her. Submitted. He melted into her presence as if he had been searching for her all along.

But the connection wasn't just the bond. This wasn't instinct.

I saw it. What most would miss.

Magic.

A thread of it, faint as breath, stretched from her fingertips to the pup's brow. It curled around him like a whisper, then melted into his chest in a pulse of light I felt more than saw. Ancient.

That didn't make her human.

It made her something else.

She is a magical being.

It is the very thing that we, the Gunnolf, were raised to avoid—taught to fear and run from. This is a presence capable of tearing apart entire kingdoms. My great-grandfather sparked an entire war for this reason. All it took was one magical being. That's all it took.

And now she was here.

She was here, in my world.

She had been in my arms just days ago.

I watched her carefully, silently. My heart pounded fiercely within my chest. I wanted to believe she was different. And maybe she was. I'd seen cold ones before—the sharp, manipulative types who wielded their magic like a blade. But Liliam was soft. Gentle. She was the kind of soul that soothed the wounded instead of creating them.

And clearly, the pup knew it.

He trembled once, then leaned into her touch with the kind of aching relief that made my breath catch. It was like he'd finally found the safety he didn't know he needed.

A shiver crawled up my spine.

Liliam's hand brushed over his head again, and the air around her shifted. The shift was not a dazzling, spark-filled explosion, but rather a more subdued one. The shift was of a far older nature. I felt it behind my eyes. There was a subtle hum that resonated deep within my bones. Like a spell being remembered.

She wasn't just comforting the pup.

She was anchoring him. Healing him. And maybe—without realizing—healing herself.

"I felt something," she whispered, her voice trembling as her eyes stayed locked on the small body in her arms. "I don't know what it was, but when I touched him... it was like something inside me answered."

I swallowed hard, forcing my expression to remain calm. I couldn't let it show. My heartbeat quickened, and my instincts cried out in alarm. I understood the significance of that.

She didn't.

And maybe—for now—that was a blessing.

"He's just scared," I said quietly, carefully. "You're calm. He feels that."

I crafted a lie that was both safe and truthful, ensuring she didn't become defensive.

She looked down again, and I watched the same delicate weave form around the pup, like threads of warmth and wildness curling around them both, like a cradle. The forest appeared to have recognized her presence.

My heart pounded with a sense of caution. If she ever found out what she truly was—what this meant—it would change everything. It would alter the perception that others held of her. She had a new perspective on herself. It might even take her away from me.

I wasn't ready for that.

So, I crouched beside her, letting my voice drop low. "You have a gift, Liliam."

She didn't lift her head. Too focused on the pup. But I saw the way she held him—arms protective, fingers splayed gently across his back. She held him as if he had been hers forever. Maybe he had.

I reached out slowly and brushed my knuckles down the pup's spine. He didn't flinch. Didn't growl. He just leaned into the touch, sighing like he was home.

"You're not just comforting him," I murmured.

You're awakening something deep within all of us.

She didn't let go. Even when the tremors stopped. Even when the pup curled deeper into her arms like she was the only thing keeping him whole—she stayed right there. She cradled him as if she had done so in a previous life.

I couldn't look away.

Her movements were soft, measured, and instinctive. Her fingers threaded behind his ears with a tenderness that seemed to steady the very air around us. Her breathing finally slowed, as if holding him had somehow anchored her.

Gaius, the restless creature in my soul, had gone quiet.

"Chosen," he whispered.

And he was right. I should've told her then. I should have spoken the truth.

But how do you tell someone they might not be entirely human? Could it be that their blood is infused with the spirits of long-forgotten gods? These entities evoke fear in people. Worship. Or try to destroy.

How can you tell someone you love that they possess qualities that could incite wars?

So, I didn't.

I remained near, my heart pounding, fervently hoping that I would have enough time to shield her from her true nature. I also feared the consequences of the world's discovery. So instead, I said the one thing I knew I could.

"You should keep him."

She blinked, looking up at me like I'd just spoken another language. "What?"

I nodded toward the pup still burrowed into her lap. "You should keep him. Take care of him."

Her brows knit together. "Zeff... I can't just take in a wild wolf pup."

"He's not wild anymore," I said gently. "Not to you."

Her mouth opened and then closed again.

I could see the doubt forming in the way her eyes flicked. "What if he needs a pack?"

I hesitated, then met her gaze. "He just found one."

She scrutinized my face as if she were deciphering hidden meanings, and perhaps she did. Maybe she felt it too, even if she couldn't name it.

"I don't know the first thing about raising a wolf," she said, her voice quieter now.

"You'll learn," I said with a shrug, keeping my voice light. "Honestly, I think he'll do most of the teaching."

She looked back down, her fingers brushing through his scruffy fur. The pup gave a small sigh and shifted, tucking his tiny nose against her chest.

He'd already decided.

"He's not going to leave you, Liliam," I said softly. "And I don't think you want him to."

She didn't answer, but she didn't deny it either.

After a pause, she murmured, "He's perfect, isn't he?"

I smiled. "He takes after his new mom."

That response earned me a look—a half-glare, half-flush that made something warm settle in my chest.

She held the pup a little tighter. "If I keep him… he needs a name."

I tilted my head. "Any ideas?"

She glanced down again, her fingers stroking along his back. "Shadow," she said softly. "Because he found me in the dark… and I didn't feel alone anymore."

My throat tightened.

Shadow.

Yeah. That felt right.

"Shadow," I repeated, nodding.

She smiled, and it reached her eyes this time. It was soft, tired, but real.

In that moment, I knew—without a doubt—that she wasn't just taking care of the broken little soul she cradled as if he had always been hers.

She was healing something in herself, too.

The pup—Shadow, now—was fast asleep in her arms by the time we returned to the cottage.

He looked so small as he curled against her chest, with his tiny ears twitching every so often while we stepped through the door. She moved carefully, as if afraid she might wake him—or worse, drop him—but her grip was secure. Natural. It felt as though he was meant to be there.

She sat down gently on the bed, still wrapped in my flannel, her hair mussed from the forest wind, her cheeks still pink from the cold.

I couldn't help but smile.

I crouched near the fire, feeding it with a few more logs. The flames jumped to life, casting the room in flickering gold, chasing away the last of the chill.

"You know he's probably going to sleep like that for hours," I said, glancing back at her.

She gave me a soft, almost apologetic smile. "I would rather not wake him."

I stood and leaned against the edge of the bed, arms crossed. "Well, that makes two of us. He looks pretty damn comfortable."

She looked down at the pup and chuckled. "He does. But he's not the one I'm worried about."

I tilted my head. "No?"

Her eyes flicked to me, and she sighed. "Owen."

Ah.

Right. Him.

The name dropped like a stone in the warmth between us.

She shifted, her arms tightening slightly around Shadow. "He's been… off lately. This? Is bringing a wolf pup into the house a beneficial idea? He's going to flip."

I tried to keep my voice even. "You're not doing this for him, are you?"

She blinked, then looked away. "No. But he's still my—" She paused, her throat bobbing. "He's still part of my life."

I nodded slowly, attempting to keep Gaius from surfacing at the mere mention of the guy.

"Well," I said, tone light, "just tell him you found a helpless orphaned pup in the woods, and your coworker was useless and insisted you raise it."

She laughed. "That's not entirely untrue."

"I'll take full blame. I'll even send him a voice memo in my 'this-was-all-me' tone."

She snorted. "He'd hate your tone."

I smirked. "Most people do. It's part of my charm."

She rolled her eyes, but I saw the way the corners of her mouth pulled up again. That tension she carried with Owen—it never sat right on her. Like wearing someone else's jacket: too tight, too worn in all the wrong places.

"What if he tells me to get rid of him?" she asked suddenly, her voice quiet.

I sat beside her, careful not to disturb the bundle of fur between us. "Then you don't listen."

She looked at me, searching my face. "It's not that simple."

"It should be," I said, gentler now. "You're allowed to care about something—even if it's inconvenient. Even if someone else doesn't get it."

Her eyes dropped to Shadow. He gave a soft snuffle in his sleep, his tiny nose pressed into her chest. Silence hung between us, but it wasn't heavy. It was warm. Close.

"I'm screwed, aren't I?" She eventually said this while smiling in a tired, amused way.

I leaned back on my palms. "Totally."

She looked at me again, her expression unreadable. "Thank you, Zeff."

"For what?"

"For... this. I am grateful for everything. You were not obligated to pursue me. Alternatively, assist me. Or let me steal a wolf."

I grinned. "Oh, I had to help you steal the wolf. You were doing it all wrong."

Her eyes sparkled, and for a moment, the only sound was the soft crackle of the fire and the quiet breathing of the pup between us.

And for the first time since I met her, she looked like she wasn't running from something.

9
THE PUP

Liliam

The house had grown used to the quiet in Owen's absence in such a short time. Shadow had filled the silence in a way Owen hadn't for months—small paws padding across the floor, soft breaths at my side as I slept, the warmth of something that didn't expect anything from me. Someone desired my proximity.

We'd found a rhythm. And in that silence, I'd finally started to breathe again.

Shadow had discovered the ideal spot to rest—curled up at my hip, as if he were meant to be there. His soft, dark gray fur rose and fell in a slow, steady rhythm, each breath a lullaby. I couldn't resist running my fingers gently along his back, and each time I did, he leaned into the touch with a quiet, contented sigh.

He was definitely a pup—but not in the way most people would imagine. Compared to a regular dog, Shadow was already the size of a full-grown Toy Fox Terrier. Compact, yes. But powerful.

After our little hiking episode—complete with unexpected howls and terrifying eyes in the dark—I'd spent hours reading up on wolves. Articles. Forums. Even outdated research papers were available. I wanted to make sure I was doing right by him.

Zeff, ever the practical one, had simply said, "Give him plenty of protein."

But that didn't ease my anxiety. Shadow wasn't just any pup. He was a wild wolf pup. Would it be appropriate to take him to a vet?

Once, I voiced the suggestion aloud, giving it a thorough thought. And I swear, Shadow gave me the most judging look I'd ever seen on a living creature. Head slightly tilted, golden eyes narrowed just enough to make me second-guess my entire train of thought.

"Can you even understand me?" I'd muttered, eyeing him suspiciously.

He blinked.

Then yawned.

He placed one paw on my thigh, displaying a possessive demeanor.

I stared down at him, fingers still absentmindedly stroking his fur. "You're not just a pup, are you?" I whispered.

Shadow didn't move at first. He kept breathing in that steady, sleepy rhythm. But then, with a quiet huff, he lifted his head and met my gaze squarely.

He didn't look like a dog.

Like a person.

There was something different in his eyes—too knowing, too calm. I'd read somewhere that wolves don't hold eye contact unless they mean it. And Shadow? He wasn't just holding it. He was searching.

I shifted, a shiver running down my spine despite the warmth in the room. "Okay… that's unsettling."

He blinked slowly. Then, he did something that completely froze me.

With deliberate precision, Shadow raised one paw and tapped it gently against the browser page I've been reading on my tablet. I'd been scrolling through for hours. I had left the page about wolf behavior and dominance cues open. He tapped it once. Then twice. His golden eyes never left mine.

"Are you—" I swallowed hard. "Are you trying to tell me something?"

The paw returned to my leg.

I stared at the tablet, then at him. "Okay," I muttered, dragging in a breath. "I'm officially losing my mind."

Now, what came next made my heart stutter. As soon as I heard the lock turn and the quiet push of the front door, I knew who it was.

Owen.

Owen walked with a measured and familiar stride. The kind he used when he didn't want to wake me—when he still cared to tiptoe around my rest.

But tonight, I wasn't sleeping.

I didn't even sit up as he reached the bedroom. The door creaked open.

He stood there in the doorway, suitcase still in hand, his eyes scanning the room until they landed on me. His shoulders eased just slightly—until his gaze dropped.

On Shadow.

His jaw tightened. "What the fuck is that, Liliam?"

I sat up quickly, shielding the pup without realizing it. Shadow blinked, ears twitching, already sensing the storm.

"He's a pup," I said, keeping my voice even. "I found him in the forest. I couldn't leave him."

Owen stepped inside, and annoyance crossed his brown eyes. "You brought a wolf into our home?"

"He's not a threat—"

"He's a damn wolf, Liliam! Wolves eat meat."

"So do dogs."

"Dogs eat commercialized food!"

Shadow gave a low growl, small and shaky, but the warning was there. It was the first time I'd heard him growl since I picked him up. I rested my hand gently on his back. "Easy," I whispered, more to Owen than Shadow. "He's not dangerous."

"You don't know that," Owen snapped. "He's a wild animal. You've lost your mind." Owen's glare darkened. "Get rid of it."

My spine straightened. "No."

His mouth fell open. "No?"

"He's staying."

"You always do this," he growled. "You never think. You never ask. You just decide."

"I had to," I said quietly. "He was alone. And I couldn't leave him."

Owen took a step closer. Shadow stiffened beneath my hand.

"You don't even know how to take care of it," Owen spat. "Where'd you even find it?"

But his eyes narrowed as if he was thinking, "Why were you in the forest? You always say you hate going there."

I hesitated. That was a mistake.

Owen's eyes darkened. "Don't tell me. Let me guess. Zeff."

I swallowed. "He was there, but—"

"Of course he was," Owen snapped, his voice sharp enough to slice through the air. "You go on some little nature walk with your work apprentice and bring home a wolf. Are you aware of how that sounds, Liliam? That sounds insane."

"You're being jealous—"

"Of course I'm jealous, Liliam!" he exploded. "My girlfriend's out playing wilderness games with another man while I'm halfway across the city. You disappear for hours and come back smelling like him."

I stiffened. I was shocked to find myself smelling like him. My pulse quickened, the memory of the dream flickering like embers across my skin. The heat. The hunger. Zeff's hands had left a mark on me, but it wasn't real; it was a dream. Just a dream…

"Nothing is going on," I said, trying to keep my voice even.

He laughed bitterly. "Bullshit."

"The pup needed help," I continued, ignoring the spike in my throat. "And Zeff—"

"Oh, I'm sure he needed help from you." His lip curled as he stepped forward. "I bet you were really generous with it."

My blood ran cold.

"And what if I was?" I snapped before I could stop myself; I rose to my feet. "He takes care of me."

That's rich, Liliam. One kiss, and now you're dreaming about him bending you over every surface in the forest.

Owen's face twisted, fury blooming in his eyes. "You think that's care?" he snarled. "He's circling like a mutt, waiting for scraps. And you're handing them out like he's earned them."

"And you're what, Owen?" My voice trembled, not with fear, but with the sheer weight of everything I'd kept buried. "A man who disappears for days, who cheats, and comes back expecting to find everything just where he left it? You don't get to talk about loyalty."

Silence. For a moment, it was like the world held its breath. Then his jaw tightened, and his fists curled so tightly that the veins in his forearms bulged. "You're pushing it."

"No," I said, quieter now, but solid. "You pushed it. And now you're angry because I stopped stepping back."

A muscle in his cheek twitched. He stood there, frozen in place. And then—he turned.

"If that thing causes any problems," he growled, voice low and venomous, "it's gone. I don't care what kind of sob story you bought with it. I mean it."

He didn't wait for an answer. The door slammed hard enough to rattle the windows. The room echoed with the absence of him. The fury he left behind still hummed through the walls, sharp and metallic like blood on steel.

Shadow whimpered softly.

He nudged closer, pressing against my leg like he felt every bit of it—every crack, every bruise, every breath I was trying to hold in. My hand found his fur, trembling.

"I'm sorry," I whispered to no one in particular. "I don't even know who I'm apologizing to anymore."

But Shadow just leaned closer.

I curled my body around the pup, burying my face in his soft fur.

Shadow had drifted off beside me again, little paws twitching in sleep. But my eyes stared at the ceiling, heavy with everything that had just happened.

The sound of Owen's voice still rang in my ears. His anger. His disbelief. Something flashed behind his eyes, frightening me even without him raising a hand.

But tonight, I hadn't flinched.

I'd chosen Shadow.

And part of me... felt guilty.

The other part?

Free.

My phone buzzed softly on the nightstand. I blinked, startled. It was past midnight.

Zeff sent me a message.

Zeff:

Are you okay?

Simple. But it carried weight. He appeared to be aware of it. I stared at it for a moment, fingers hovering over the screen. My chest tightened.

Another buzz ensued.

Zeff:

I would rather not assume anything. I was just checking in.

A shaky breath escaped me. Of course, he felt something. Zeff always noticed the things I tried to bury.

And then, one last message:

Zeff:

If you need to talk—or just want to sit in silence with someone who gets it—I'm around. You don't have to be alone tonight, so please reach out if you need support.

I didn't reply right away.

Instead, I pressed the screen to my chest, allowing the tears to finally fall—quiet and hot, not from pain this time, but from the recognition.

I glanced down at Shadow, still curled up against me, and whispered, "Maybe we're both lucky."

Then I typed back.

Me:
I'm okay now. Thanks to you.
I also want to express my gratitude to Shadow.
But... can we talk tomorrow?

The reply came almost instantly:

Zeff:
Anytime.

I walked over to my closet, where Zeff's flannel from our hiking trip lay tucked away. He'd refused to take it back that night he walked me home, muttering something about how it looked better on me anyway.

I picked it up, inhaling the lingering traces of his scent—coffee with a mix of wood smoke and pine.

Pulling it over my head, I smiled.

Tonight, I was going to sleep feeling cozy.

****

Over the coming days, Owen barely spoke to me.

Again.

We moved through the apartment like ghosts—two strangers under one roof, orbiting the same space but never touching. Our conversations, if they happened at all, were mechanical. Functional. "Pass the salt." "The rent cleared." "Your phone buzzed."

It felt like living with a roommate who didn't care to remember my name.

The only time we shared more than a wall was during the silent, tension-thick car rides to and from work. He'd grip the wheel tightly, jaw clenched, eyes on the road like I wasn't even there. Occasionally I'd glance over, hoping to find a crack in his expression. A sign that he still saw me.

But there was nothing.

Shadow, on the other hand, was a constant presence. Shadow served as my silent guardian. The little wolf pup followed me everywhere—with unwavering loyalty and a sharp sense of awareness that didn't match his age or size. He even waited at the bathroom door, ears perked, tail curled neatly around him. But he never looked. Not once.

If I took a shower, he would sit on the rug near the tub, eyes respectfully averted until I wrapped a towel around myself. When I dressed, he'd turn his back, tail flicking with exaggerated disinterest like a chivalrous knight bound by an unspoken code.

Some days, I felt like Shadow had more respect than most of the men I'd ever met.

His presence became my comfort, even as Owen's irritation with him grew sharper, visible in every roll of his eyes, every passive-aggressive sigh when Shadow curled at my feet. I caught him muttering under his breath more than once, but I never asked what he said.

I didn't want to know.

Still, I couldn't shake the feeling that Shadow knew things. Felt things. His intelligence wasn't just surprising—it was uncanny. His glances lingered longer than they should, his posture tense at the exact moments my thoughts turned dark. He wasn't just reacting.

He was understanding.

And that frightened me more than I wanted to admit.

I couldn't help but wonder, what else could he perceive?

In the short span of days that Shadow had been with me, I noticed something strange—something that refused to be explained by vet blogs or late-night Google spirals. He was growing.

He was not developing as a typical puppy would. This was sudden. Subtle. It was as if a quiet magic was blossoming in his bones.

His legs were longer. His paws were more solid. His spine straightened. Every morning, I would find myself lingering for a little longer, questioning whether I was imagining it or if the world was deceiving me.

Especially after the morning in the kitchen—the one where Shadow growled at Owen without hesitation. Low. Protective. Unapologetic.

That day, I tried to keep my routine steady. Familiar. I needed a solid foundation as the boundaries of my surroundings continued to change.

Wake up. Coffee. Shadow's food. Avoid the man pacing the living room like a ghost trying to remember the shape of his name.

By the time I arrived at the office, I was exhausted. Emotionally fried. My chest was tight, my skin overstimulated. I moved through the day like a shadow—answering emails, sorting files, and smiling when prompted. Every so often, someone would mention the "adorable little wolf pup" they'd seen on social media. I'd force a laugh and downplay it. Avoid the reality.

Zeff was… different.

He didn't push.He didn't pry.

He'd just offer a cup of coffee, his voice like warm velvet. "Shadow okay?" He'd ask softly, eyes holding mine just long enough to remind me I wasn't invisible.

It wasn't Owen helping me navigate new routines. It wasn't Owen who noticed the quiet bags under my eyes, the way I clutched my phone like it held me together. It wasn't Owen showing up with things that made life easier.

It was Zeff. Always, Zeff.

He would appear at our work in the morning with a canvas bag slung over his shoulder—filled with high-protein kibble, two soft chew toys, and a fleece blanket that smelled faintly of pine.

"Figured you could use one less thing to worry about," he said, laying everything out like it was the most natural thing in the world.

Then he smiled slowly and said, "Since I'm the adopted father now."

I laughed—genuinely this time—and slapped his arm playfully, the contact sparking something I tried not to name. My hand lingered a beat too long.

When I came home, the weight of the day still clung to my skin like damp clothes I couldn't peel off. But the moment I sank to the floor beside Shadow, some of it slipped away.

He was already tugging one of the new toys from Zeff's canvas bag, tiny teeth gripping it with a determination that made my chest ache.

Owen would've never done this.

I would've never noticed the shift in my shoulders. He would never have guessed my needs without my explicit request.

Shadow let out a soft huff of satisfaction and collapsed on the rug, paws curled around the toy, his tail wagging with a lazy, content rhythm. His joy was quiet. Trusting. Complete.

And me?

I sat there in silence, still in awe of how simple it was to see. Taken care of. I experienced the tiniest, purest kind of love. without anticipation.

I reached into the bag, starting to unpack the rest of the supplies, mind wandering—but something small caught my eye, tucked deep in the corner, hidden beneath the edge of a folded blanket.

It was a black velvet pouch.

My brows knit as I picked it up, loosening the drawstring. Something shifted inside—a soft slide. I tilted the pouch, and a tiny box fell into my palm. Delicate. Smooth. It felt cool to the touch.

Inside was a necklace. Simple. Perfect.

The necklace was a slender chain, with a finely carved wolf pendant at its center, its head thrown back mid-howl. Tiny runes laced its fur, subtle but deliberate, and when I moved it beneath the lamp's glow, they shimmered faintly, catching the light like breath.

When my fingers brushed the wolf's shape, something flickered under my skin. A ripple. A hum. The air around me felt warmer. Denser.

I found a small slip of parchment nestled beneath the box. Just three words, penned in Zeff's sharp, deliberate hand:

For protection. Always.

My throat closed. Something in me cracked open—wide and raw.

Shadow stirred beside me, as if he felt it too. He lifted his head, ears twitching, eyes meeting mine. And then, as if to say, "You're not alone," his tail thumped once against the floor.

My fingers curled around the pendant, pressing it to my chest. The metal was cool—but it pulsed like a second heartbeat.

And for the first time in a long while, I felt it.

Even though no one had expressed it explicitly yet, I felt safe.

****

Zeff

The study's walls were covered in long, flowing shadows as the fire crackled softly in the hearth. The air smelled like iron and ash and old parchment and burned pine. The only sounds in the room were the soft, repetitive tapping of the pen between my fingers against the open book in front of me and the faint hiss of wood cracking in the flames.

I hadn't asked permission to take it.

Getting this volume out of the Archives of the Reservoir had required discretion, a little charm, and a name that still carried weight in places that mattered. I hadn't dared ask one of the elders for assistance. That would've raised too many questions. There were too many onlookers. And I didn't need the kind of whispers that followed curiosity.

Being Alpha had its perks.

Still, even now, I felt the weight of the text staring back at me—its worn leather binding etched with ancient symbols, some faded, others still sharp enough to sting if touched carelessly. Old bloodlines. Old power. The warnings dated back even further.

I leaned back in the chair, dragging a hand through my hair and exhaling slowly. The room, despite the fire, felt colder than it should've.

This morning, I'd seen her wearing the necklace.

My necklace.

It had been subtle—tucked just beneath the collar of her blouse, the delicate silver chain disappearing into the hollow of her throat. But the pendant… The pendant had rested square against her collarbone, glinting softly when she moved, bearing the mark of my bloodline. A wolf mid-howl, runes curling through its fur, like whispers from another time.

I'd had to call in a favor from Brogan to get it forged—faster than I liked, with fewer questions than he was comfortable with. Brogan never did like keeping secrets, especially not from me. However, sharing the information was out of the question. Not yet.

If the tome was right—and Goddess help me, I think it is—then that necklace, woven with the smallest trace of my wolf's blood, should help keep her magic soothed. Balanced. This should continue until she feels ready.

But fuck.

If I'm right… If she is what I suspect, she is…

Then I must tread carefully. Very carefully.

The last time a Gunnolf attempted to bind a magical being to secure a second chance at mating, that action initiated a war that nearly led to destruction.

I will not repeat that mistake.

She must choose me. Freely. Without magic. Without pressure. Without fear.

Because if she is what I think she is—

Then she's not just my mate. She's a key to something ancient.

I leaned back in my chair, the leather groaning beneath me as I exhaled through my nose, rubbing the tension from my jaw. My hands were trembling again, a quiet tremor I only ever felt after being near her. That pulse of energy—hers—crackled against my skin like static. But it wasn't just desire. It was something deeper. Pure.

When I touched her... I felt power. Ancient. Dormant. Untapped.

Something is sleeping in human skin. But she didn't know it yet.

And gods, what will happen the moment she realizes it?

I could still feel her warmth lingering on my fingertips. That accidental brush of skin when she passed me the folder earlier today... It had nearly undone me. I felt her magic then— buried deep, wild, and coiled like a sleeping beast. It didn't frighten me.

It called to me. And it terrified me... because I wanted it. Her.

It was not because the bond was gnawing at me as if it were already halfway formed. It wasn't because my heart ached every time she smiled.

She fueled my desire for more. She made me yearn for more.

The door creaked open behind me, and I didn't need to look to know it was Josh. I instantly picked up the old tome and placed it in one of the drawers of my desk.

John My beta. My second. He was also my oldest friend.

"You're going to kill yourself at this pace," Josh said flatly, his voice scraped raw from fatigue and that quiet, simmering judgment only he could deliver without raising it.

He didn't need to yell to make it sting.

Josh's posture was always that of a soldier, his shoulders squared with purpose, his movements sharp and calculated, as if his body had memorized a battlefield long ago. The close-cropped dark hair, the unrelenting jaw, and those brown eyes—they were designed to cut through anything soft. Including me.

He stood in the doorway for a beat before stepping into the room. The floorboards creaked under his boots—three strides, and he was at my desk.

I didn't lift my head. "The pack still needs—"

"They don't need a dead Alpha," he cut in, firmer now.

He placed a thick hand on the edge of the desk, fingers splayed like he might crush the damn wood if I argued.

"You've barely slept since last week. You're working double shifts—running strategy here and pretending to be human out there. You think no one notices? We do."

I finally met his eyes. He didn't flinch. He never did.

"I'm fine," I said. It wasn't even convincing for me.

"You're not," he snapped. "You're stretched thin, Zeff. You are expending energy as if you have nothing left to lose. And for what? Are you trying to become a one-man war machine? You're trying to carry the weight of the pack and her world. Alone. Without letting anyone help you."

That landed harder than it should have.

Josh didn't say her name, but we both felt it settle between us like thunder waiting to strike.

I opened my mouth to deny it—then closed it again.

What was I supposed to say?

That I couldn't breathe right unless I knew she was safe?

That I'd gladly tear my soul apart holding two lives together if it meant she didn't have to?

Every time I saw her smile at Shadow or run her fingers along that wolf pendant at her throat, I felt a flicker of hope so dangerous I didn't know whether to chase it or run.

I said nothing, jaw locked tight against everything I didn't know how to name.

Josh's voice dropped, low and pointed. "You're afraid of what happens if she chooses you."

That pierced something I didn't expect. Not a wound—but the space where a wound had tried to heal.

"I'm afraid," I murmured, "of what happens if she doesn't."

Josh blinked, the shift in his expression quiet but undeniable. It was as if he hadn't even considered that fear before.

I stared down at my hands—calloused, scarred, capable of both violence and tenderness. They flexed restlessly, clenching and unclenching as if trying to hold something invisible.

"She must have a choice," I said. "She must. I won't chain her to me just because the moon carved it into our bones. I'm not going to be like them—those alphas who claim and mark and bind just to quiet the hunger inside."

Josh exhaled, slow and steady. His stance eased. "You're not them."

"She deserves to choose her fate," I said again, softer this time. "Not be dragged into it because the gods or the bloodlines decided she was mine."

Silence lingered between us like a held breath.

Then Josh stepped forward, placing a folder gently on the edge of the desk.

"She's wearing the necklace," he said quietly. "That's something."

But I didn't answer. I couldn't. My mind was already spinning ahead—to the moment she would learn the truth. I couldn't stop thinking about the bond we shared. She will discover the truth about who I truly am. It's about the essence of her.

She'll run.

Or worse—she'll stay out of guilt. She may do so out of a sense of duty. She may be acting out of a misguided sense of protection.

And I couldn't bear that.

I didn't want her compliance. I didn't want her pity. I didn't want her out of fear.

I wanted her laughter. Her chaos. Her stubbornness. Her fire.

I wanted her to have me. A desire that wasn't dictated by fate. But because she did,.

Josh turned, walking halfway to the door before pausing. He looked back over his shoulder, his voice gentler now.

"You don't have to carry this burden alone, Zeff. Let her in. Before someone else does."

I didn't respond.

I simply gazed at my hands once more, still buzzing with the recollection of her touch

****

She lay beside me in the grass, her body bathed in golden light as the sunlight filtered through the canopy. Her dress—a pale, delicate thing that clung to her like breath—draped over her hips, tracing every gentle curve. The breeze teased the hem, coaxing it to sway just enough to make me ache. Her dark hair spilled behind her, a river of black silk against the green, glinting like obsidian in the sun.

She turned her head to look at me, those amber eyes soft and searching, as if I were the only thing in the world that made sense. A blade of grass caught against her thigh, bending in worship. Her lips parted slightly, like she was about to speak—

And for once, the present wasn't one of those scorching, erotic dreams that left me cursing the waking world and desperate for the real thing. No. This… this felt pure. Whole. Almost holy.

"Zeff," she whispered, my name slipping from her mouth like a promise.

I reached for her, fingers poised to tuck a strand of hair behind her ear—

But then the light faltered.

A shadow slithered in, coiling like smoke, creeping with intent. Before I could react, it wrapped around her wrists like dark fingers, yanking her away with a gasp and a flash of panic in her eyes.

"Liliam!" I surged to my feet, the forest exploding into chaos. Fog poured in from all sides, heavy and unnatural. I pushed through it, heart thundering, breath ragged. It was like sprinting through a nightmare I knew too well—always behind, always too late.

Then, she emerged from the mist.

She stood in a clearing, ringed by alpha wolves. Alpha wolves, with their glowing eyes and bristling fur, towered over her. But she wasn't afraid. Her skin glowed with a golden hue, radiant and defiant, like a goddess on the cusp of war. Her hair whipped around her in an unseen wind, her dress clinging to her like she was born of light and storm.

Behind her, the shadows took shape—massive, hulking, and hungry. Two crimson eyes blinked open in the black. A voice like rusted metal scraped through the trees:

"You are not the only one who sees her."

The wolves circled, growling low. Her scent, once sweet like blooming blackberries, was tainted, now drenched in the iron tang of blood. My gut twisted. Her power was humming, awakening, attracting things I couldn't protect her from.

Come with me, I tried to say. Please. But the words caught like thorns in my throat.

I reached for her—desperate, wild—

She stepped back.

Her golden eyes locked on mine. Fear. Pain. Anger. "Don't lie to me, Zeff."

The shadows lunged. A snarl. A blur of black and red—

I woke with a violent gasp, heart pounding like a war drum. My elbow knocked the cold, forgotten coffee mug from my desk. It shattered against the floor, porcelain shards scattering like bone.

I sat there, gasping, soaked in sweat. The fire had died. The study was dark. But the fear in my chest—that was alive. Cold. Real.

The dream had become more than just a fantasy. Could it mean she was waking up?

And if I wasn't careful—if I hesitated for even one second—someone else might reach her first.

And for the first time in my life, I wasn't just afraid of losing her. I was afraid of losing everything she could have been—with me.

The hand of fate was merely guiding me. She wasn't guaranteed.

****

Liliam

As dawn gently broke over the forest, the trees rustled around me, their leaves whispering secrets I would rather not hear. The sky bled pale gold through the branches, casting streaks of light over the mist-cloaked path. The air was thick with dew and something else—something unspoken.

I didn't know how I'd gotten here. The world appeared muted and suspended. Like the forest was holding its breath.

The ground beneath my boots felt familiar—too familiar. The damp soil, the occasional crunch of a twig, and the brush of cool mist curling around my legs were all familiar. My body moved on instinct, every step drawing me deeper into something I wasn't sure I could escape.

And then I smelled it.

It was the aroma of freshly brewed coffee. Rich. Bold. Laced with dark chocolate. His signature.

My breath caught mid-step. My pulse stuttered.

I turned, and there he was.

Zeff.

Barefoot at the edge of the reservoir, his bare chest catching the amber light like a painting come to life. Every muscle etched in soft, brutal beauty. His hair still damp, jaw sharp, his green eyes locked onto mine like he'd been waiting—forever.

He looked like sin carved out of starlight. And I... I couldn't move.

"Liliam," he said, voice deep, thick with sleep—or lust.

"I shouldn't be here," I whispered. But I didn't mean it. My feet moved anyway. My body betrayed me. Or maybe it told the truth I'd tried so hard to hide.

Step by step, the space between us dissolved. The air vibrated with something primal.

When I reached him, the heat coming off his body seeped into mine like a brand. His hand came up, slow and deliberate, brushing a lock of hair from my cheek. His fingertips scorched my skin.

His eyes dragged over my face like he was memorizing it. His voice dipped low. "Were you following me?"

"No," I breathed, lips parting. "I was running."

"Toward me," he murmured, leaning in. "Always toward me."

The tip of his nose grazed my temple, his breath ghosting across my skin like silk. "I can smell you," he whispered. "The way you ache. Your need. It's beautiful."

I shuddered. Not out of fear but out of want. And then his mouth brushed mine. Feather-light. Barely there. It was a question.

I answered it with fire.

I surged forward, kissing him like I needed him to breathe.

He caught me in one fluid motion, his arms locking around my waist as our mouths crashed again, deeper, hungrier.

God, the way he kissed—like he was starving for me. He treated me as if I were water, having spent years in the desert.

His hand slid up my back, under my shirt, and every inch of my skin that met his fingers came alive, aching. My nails dug into his shoulders, needing more. I craved his entire presence.

Zeff growled into my mouth—a low, primal sound that curled between my thighs and made my knees buckle. His thigh slid between mine, and I moaned.

He didn't stop.

"You feel it too," he rasped against my lips.

"Yes," I gasped. "I feel it."

"I've been good," he said. "So fucking good. But I dream of you every damn night. Just like this."

He kissed me again—rougher, deeper—like he needed to mark me. My body arched into him, and his hands claimed me, possessive and reverent all at once.

He lowered us to the forest floor, the moss soft beneath my back. The sky above turned molten gold. His body blanketed mine, his weight perfect, grounding me and setting me on fire all at once.

He hovered just above me, his lips brushing my throat. "Say it," he demanded, his voice like thunder wrapped in silk.

"I'm yours," I whispered, trembling.

He growled, satisfied. "Mine."

And God help me, I was.

He parted his lips and sank his teeth into the curve of my neck.

I woke with a violent gasp, heart pounding, skin slick with heat. My sheets tangled around me like chains. The scent of coffee lingered on my skin like a ghost.

Shadow lay curled at my feet, his ears twitching. He stirred slightly, sensing something in me.

I pressed a trembling hand to my chest. My lips still tingled. The dream clung to me like humidity, thick and intimate. Zeff's hands, mouth, and voice felt incredibly genuine.

I glanced at the time. 3:47 AM.

It seemed too early to be true.

It was too late to pretend that I didn't want it.

I turned onto my side, eyes wide open, and whispered into the quiet, "What the hell is happening to me?"

And deep in my chest…

I already knew the answer. I barely slept after the dream.

Every time I closed my eyes, I felt his mouth on mine. I heard his voice in my ear. I felt the pressure of his body above me, surrounding me, claiming me.

By the time I managed to wake up with Shadow, the morning light filtered through the kitchen window, casting soft shadows across the room. I moved around, gathering ingredients to make breakfast, my mind half on the tasks ahead for the day. Shadow was right at my heels, following my every step like a little shadow of his own. He'd become my constant companion, and I couldn't help but smile at his devotion.

"Shadow, you're going to trip me," I teased, nudging him gently with my foot as I reached for the eggs. With his tail wagging and his eyes bright, he watched my every move, seemingly understanding everything I said.

I was so engrossed in my morning routine—eggs cracking into a bowl, the soft rhythm of the whisk—that I didn't hear Owen come in from his study. He moved silently, like a ghost slipping into a moment that didn't belong to him. The next sensation I experienced was the warmth of his body against my back, as his arm encircled my waist.

I gasped, nearly dropping the bowl. "Owen!"

But he didn't let me say anything more. He pulled me against him, his grip possessive, and kissed me—rough and urgent, as if trying to reclaim something already slipping through his fingers. His mouth was all pressure and insistence, lips moving with a hunger I hadn't felt from him in a long time.

It stunned me. The way he kissed me—not out of tenderness, but assertion. There was no gentleness in it, no warmth. Just a reminder: I'm still here.

My body tensed. For a heartbeat, I couldn't breathe. Couldn't think. His hands gripped my sides tighter, fingertips pressing into my skin like a brand. It didn't feel good. It didn't feel bad. It just… didn't feel like us.

I tried. I did. I kissed him back, making myself remember the boy who once knew how to hold me. The way his laugh used to melt me. I remembered the quiet nights when I believed this was it—this was safety. But it all felt too far away now, like flipping through a memory that belonged to someone else.

And then, like a cruel whisper in my mind, Zeff surfaced.

His voice dipped as he uttered my name. He gazed at me with a sense of sanctity and forbiddingness simultaneously. His touch was not a claim but rather an invitation.

My heart stuttered.

Guilt rushed in like a tide, crashing through my chest and choking the breath from my lungs. What was I doing? Why was I thinking about another man—him—when Owen was right here, trying?

But my body already knew. It didn't ache for the kiss I was in. It ached for the other one.

A low growl rumbled from below. Shadow, who had been patiently watching, was now bristling, his small body tense. His growl intensified, a protective, almost feral sound that caused my heart to race.

Owen pulled back, breaking the kiss with a look of irritation. "Is that thing growling at me?" he asked, his voice laced with annoyance as he glanced down at Shadow.

I looked down at Shadow, his teeth bared, his little body tense as if ready to pounce. "Shadow, no," I said softly, trying to calm him, but his growl didn't waver. He kept his eyes on Owen, his hackles raised.

"What's wrong with him?" Owen demanded, his grip on my waist tightening. "Why does he keep doing that every time I'm near you?"

"He's just... he's protective," I tried to explain, though I wasn't sure how much sense it made. Shadow had been more sensitive to Owen's presence lately, and I couldn't quite figure out why.

Owen's expression darkened, and he released me, stepping back with a huff. "It's an animal, Liliam. You shouldn't let it act like this. You need to either train the animal or find a new home for it."

The harshness of his words stung, and I felt a wave of defensiveness rise in me. "He's not just an animal, Owen. He's been through a lot. And I'm not getting rid of him."

Owen scoffed and turned on his heel, the sound of his footsteps echoing down the hallway like a final word I would rather not hear. I watched him go, my chest tightening, a familiar weight sinking back into place where my heart used to feel steady.

Beside me, Shadow stood rigid, ears pinned, his little body still bristling with tension.

The growl in his throat had quieted—but not the warning in his stance.

I knelt slowly, fingers brushing over the soft curve of his back. "You should ease up, Shadow," I murmured, trying to coax calm into my voice.

He blinked up at me, tail twitching once… and then gave the tiniest huff, followed by a sneeze so perfectly timed it felt like a sarcastic hell no.

A breath of laughter escaped me—dry and worn out, but real.

"Yeah," I whispered, stroking his fur. "Me neither."

10
GLANCES

I had to face him.

I walked into the office like a woman heading toward her execution—each step too measured, my coat suddenly too warm despite the chill still clinging to the early morning air. Shadow had sensed it. He'd nosed at my leg before I left, pressing his little head against my knee like he wanted to anchor me in place. I'd have hated leaving him behind. Hated the thought of Owen looming around the apartment while I was gone.

The elevator pinged.

I stepped in—and froze.

Zeff was already inside.

His presence swept over me, casual, magnetic, and far too composed for the storm still brewing in my chest. He leaned against the far wall, binder in hand, jacket unzipped, and sleeves pushed up to reveal those forearms I could still feel braced on either side of me. His damp hair clung slightly at the temples, and his scent wrapped around me before I could shield myself.

"Morning," he said, easy as breath, eyes lifting to meet mine. And just like that, I wasn't in the office anymore. I was back in that dream.

His mouth against my throat. My back arched beneath him. The word "mine" seared into my skin with a reverence that makes me tremble even now.

I swallowed dryly. "Morning," I managed, though it came out thinner than I liked.

He tilted his head. "Are you okay?"

His voice was calm, but there was something under it—an edge too quiet to name

"Yeah. Fine." I jabbed the button for our floor like it might save me.

"Rough night?" he asked. I blinked. My brain stuttered.

He couldn't know. There's no way he knows.

"Sort of," I murmured, eyes fixed on the glowing floor numbers above us. I could feel him watching me.

"Hmm." His hum wasn't judgment. It was curiosity wrapped in silk. "You look a little flushed."

My heart stuttered. Blood surged hot beneath my skin

I scrambled. "I jogged. This morning. Just to wake up."

My voice cracked like splintered glass, and I hated the way his mouth curved in response—that slow, knowing smile that always felt like it stripped me bare.

The elevator doors closed.

I felt the silence stretching between us like a live wire, humming with everything unsaid.

"Jogging, huh?" Zeff finally said, tilting his head as he glanced at my outfit. "In those boots?"

Shit

I glanced down instinctively, suddenly aware of the slight heel and the very unathletic cut of my coat. "I—uh—it was more like power walking. Very determined walking."

He smirked. "Ah. The 'I'm not thinking about a man I shouldn't be thinking about' kind of walk."

My cheeks went nuclear. "That's oddly specific."

"Just a guess," he said, looking far too pleased with himself.

Gods, why did he have to smell like that? Look like that? Why does your voice make me want to pull the emergency stop and ruin us both?

I tried to laugh. Tried to play it cool. "I'm just stressed, okay? New puppy, work's a mess, Owen's—"

Don't say his name. Not in front of him.

Zeff's eyes narrowed slightly. Not judging. Just... watching.

"You don't have to explain," he said, and this time, his voice was softer. Gentler. "But... you do look tired."

I hated that he noticed.

And I hated more that I wanted him to notice.

"I'm fine," I lied. "Really."

He stepped a little closer. It was just a shift of weight, yet it felt as if gravity had tipped toward him. "You don't have to lie to me, Liliam."

My breath hitched.

You're not allowed to say my name like that. Like it tastes delicious on your tongue. Like I'm something you'd fight gods to protect.

He looked at me with that same maddening calm, but I could see the tension in his jaw. The storm he kept buried.

I remembered the storm all too well.

"You know," he said at last, "I read somewhere that when you avoid someone, it's because they matter too much."

I opened my mouth. Closed it. I reopened my mouth. "You're very full of quotes today."

He shrugged. "Maybe I just like watching you squirm."

I also enjoy the way you express yourself, as if you already know what I will do next.

The elevator chimed. We'd arrived.

I bolted forward the second the doors opened, desperate to get out, away, anywhere—but his voice followed me.

"By the way," he called after me, "you forgot your coffee."

I turned—just in time to see him hold it out.

My coffee. The one he brought me every time. The one with the smallest hint of oat milk and my absence of sugar packets.

I took it.

Our fingers brushed.

And my stupid, traitorous body sparked like it had been waiting for this single point of contact all morning.

"Thanks," I muttered, refusing to meet his eyes.

"You're welcome," he said softly.

I kept walking.

But God help me, I wanted to turn around and run back to him. These dreams were getting way too close to reality.

****

The office buzzed with its usual morning rhythm—keyboards clacking, printers humming, and the occasional ping of a Slack notification echoing across the open floor. But none of it registered.

All I could focus on was him.

Zeff.

He sat just a few feet away, his head tilted slightly as he skimmed through a printed file, his lips pursed in concentration. The exact same mouth that had kissed me breathless in my dream was now focused on the printed file. That mouth had whispered the word "mine" against my throat. That mouth had tasted to me as if I were the only thing keeping him alive.

I shook my head.

Get it together, Liliam.

But it didn't help. My eyes betrayed me, flicking back to him every few minutes, sometimes seconds. Every time he leaned forward, I caught a glimpse of his forearms flexing as he scribbled notes. Every time he pushed his chair back, the fabric of his shirt stretched across his chest in a way that made my stomach flip. And that scent—the smell I so constantly drool over—kept drifting toward me like it was hunting me

It was maddening.

At that moment, I couldn't distinguish between fantasy and reality.

Not when my body remembered the way he touched me. Not when I swore I could still feel the ghost of his hand at my waist. Not when I kept clenching my thighs under the desk, trying to control the pulse between them.

And worst of all?

He noticed.

The fourth time I looked up and caught him already looking at me, he didn't look away.

He just… smirked.

It was not a full grin, nor was it the cocky one. The smile was a subtle curve of his mouth. Slow. Dangerous.

I immediately dropped my gaze, heat crawling up my neck. I grabbed my water bottle to occupy my hands, took a long sip, and nearly choked when I noticed him still looking at me.

I cleared my throat, trying to focus on the spreadsheet in front of me.

Cell B13 displays the quarterly projections. Pivot table. Columns align—

He placed his hand on my thighs. He buried his nose deep into my neck. His fingers are dangerously close to my folds.

God. What was wrong with me?

The ache in my chest and the heat coiling low in my belly were not going away. It was getting worse. Our fingers touched each other, passing a folder between us. Every time he leaned in, his voice dipped just a little too low.

I was unraveling.

What was the most distressing part?

I didn't want it to stop.

But I couldn't act on it. I couldn't let my desire ruin what little stability I had left.

I couldn't let my desire ruin the little stability I had left, especially with Owen still at home. Not with a wolf pup curled at my feet every night. It was evident that my heart and body were no longer in sync.

I bit the inside of my cheek, hard, trying to reset my brain.

It didn't work.

Zeff let out a quiet laugh from across the room in response to something someone else said. The sound was low, rich, and unguarded. And I felt it—between my ribs, deep in my spine, in places I had no business feeling anything for anyone apart from—

"Hey."

I jumped slightly, turning to see Zeff standing beside my desk, one brow raised.

"You alright?" he asked. Voice smooth. Innocent. Too innocent.

"Yeah," I said quickly. "Fine. Just focused."

His gaze lingered a second too long. "You looked like you were somewhere else."

Yes, you were above me; your knee was next to my thigh as you shifted inside of me and moaned my name.

I forced a smile. "Just… tired."

He nodded slowly, like he didn't believe me for a second. "Are you sure? You've been kind of… twitchy."

My heart dropped into my stomach.

Twitchy? "Horny" is the word I would use.

"Maybe too much coffee," I mumbled, brushing imaginary lint from my keyboard.

His smile came back, this time with a hint of knowledge.

"Well, take a break if you need to," he said, tapping his knuckles lightly on my desk before turning and walking to his desk.

And I stared at his back.

The worst part wasn't just that I kept looking at him…

It was that part of me that wanted him to catch me. The screen blurred as I typed.

Quarterly projections indicate a 6.4% deviation from expected—my fingers slowed.

I blinked, forcing them to keep going. *—expected performance, primarily influenced by supply chain delays and—*

But the words were nothing more than symbols now. Hollow. Mechanical. My brain couldn't hold onto them. Somewhere between the terms "supply chain" and "forecasting models," I experienced the sensation once more.

The warmth of his hand swept down my spine.

His thumb gently traced the curve of my spine, slow and deliberate, as if he was trying to memorize me.

My lips parted, a breath escaping. My thighs instinctively pressed together under the desk.

I shook my head, frustrated. This wasn't helping. I had deadlines. Meetings. A perfectly normal life to uphold.

His mouth.

The way he kissed me felt like it was both the first and the last time, simultaneously devouring and reverent. It was as if he knew the places that would unravel me even before I became aware of them.

I gripped the edge of the desk, knuckles whitening. My skin prickled with the phantom of his touch, and suddenly the office was too warm. Too small. The walls seemed to encircle me.

I needed air.

The walls of the office were closing in, my thoughts spinning in an endless loop of his voice, his hands, his lips—all imagined but felt like memory.

I slipped out the side door and into the open lot behind the building. A line of trees framed the edge of the property, leaves rustling gently in the breeze. I leaned back against the brick wall, exhaling slowly, trying to breathe him out of my system.

But I couldn't.

The air out here still smelled faintly like him. It haunted me like that dream, like the way he'd looked at me earlier.

"Can't even go ten minutes without thinking about him, huh?" I muttered to myself, pressing a cold hand to my cheek.

Then came the sound of the door.

My stomach dropped. Footsteps. Familiar ones.

And then there he was.

Zeff.

His expression was unreadable at first—calm, maybe a little curious—but the moment he saw my face, something softened.

But he didn't say anything.

He stepped closer. He drew near enough for me to discern the green flecks in his eyes and the way the afternoon light caressed his cheekbones. His presence was warm and steady—like it always was.

"I would rather not push," Zeff said softly, his voice barely louder than the hum of the wind, "but if you keep looking at me like that during work hours, I might lose my job."

My breath seized in my throat.

"Zeff," I warned, but the word came out thin—shaky, almost pleading.

He smiled, with this delicious hint in his eyes. There was something heavy behind that expression. He was holding something back.

"You're not okay," he said. "I can feel it."

I swallowed. My chest tightened, a pulse fluttering beneath my ribs like a bird trying to escape its cage. "You're imagining things."

"I'm not."

I turned away, unable to meet the intensity of his gaze. It was ridiculous how quickly I unraveled around him.

The second he looked at me like that, it felt like my entire body betrayed me—as if I mattered. He perceived every aspect of me and still desired me.

"It's complicated," I muttered.

He didn't reply right away.

I turned again, finally brave enough to meet his eyes.

And that was my mistake.

I saw no smugness or cocky flirtation in them. I saw hunger. Restraint. There was a subdued desperation in his demeanor, as if he suppressed a portion of his being that could have devoured everything in its path.

He was waiting.

For me.

And suddenly, the silence between us felt too loud, too fragile. Like a match poised above gasoline.

His hand lifted, slow and steady—but he didn't touch me.

He hovered.

Knuckles trembled inches from my cheek, as if he were terrified that if he did touch me, he wouldn't be able to stop.

The space between us narrowed, charged with something electric. I inhaled, but it wasn't air I pulled into my lungs—it was him. His scent. His warmth. His pull.

God, why did I want to kiss him so badly?

Just the brush of his skin against mine had my pulse skyrocketing. I could feel it in every inch of my body, a heat blooming in my core, threatening to shatter what little control I had left. It wasn't just lust—it was gravity. Magnetic. Dangerous.

He leaned in—so close I could feel the warmth of his breath on my lips. My eyelids fluttered without meaning to, and my fingers twitched at my sides.

But he didn't kiss me.

He stepped back.

Slowly. Carefully. As if putting distance between us took all the strength he had.

"Breathe," he said, voice low, edged with something raw. "Let yourself want something without having to justify it."

Then he turned, walking back inside, leaving me there in the doorway, the sun casting light on skin that still burned for him.

And I stood there, breathless, trembling, painfully aware of one impossible truth:

I wanted him more than I wanted clarity.

11
HUNGER

I've always been stern with myself. My parents—old-fashioned and tightly preserved in their beliefs—drilled one lesson into me that stuck: Do your best. Be excellent at what you do.

While others clock out at six and return to their lives with a clean conscience, I never could. I wanted things done right. That's what earned me the workaholic label—because I stayed late by choice. I firmly believed that effort was crucial. This dedication consistently placed me on the "best employee" list.

I fell prey to my inadequacy.

It's the only thing I thank my parents for. The rest? I would've ended up a cloistered nun or a perfectly trained housewife if they'd had their way. I thanked them after graduation—then packed my things, boarded a plane, and never looked back. I chose graphic design, against their protests. I chose freedom.

I met Owen in college, and somehow… here I am. Four years later. I am doing something entirely different from what I had imagined.

Everyone else had left for the day. Except for Zeff, everyone had left for the day.

I glanced up. He was still seated across from me, flipping through a folder I'd handed him, his eyes scanning the text, brow furrowed in concentration. But I could see the fatigue—etched in the tension of his shoulders, the shadows beneath his eyes. He leaned back with a sigh, shutting his eyes briefly, shaking his head.

I know he's still here because of me.

I'd asked him to go home—twice. Maybe three times. He never answered. He just kept working beside me like he belonged there.

"Zeff—"

He set the folder down, flashing a worn-out smile. "Another round of coffee?"

I nodded softly, even though my brain barely registered the question.

I'm already addicted to everything that smells like you.

He didn't wait for an answer. He took my cold cup along with his and headed to the break room.

I bit my lower lip and glanced at the clock: 7:47 p.m. I leaned back in my chair, stretched my arms, and tried to ease the tightness creeping down my spine.

The floor room echoed with a gentle crash, then a groan. low. A little rough. inhumane.

I bolted upright. "Zeff?"

The second his name left my lips, heat bloomed through me like a slow-burning fever. It radiated outward from my chest—down to my hips, curling low in my belly. My thighs clenched instinctively. The scent hit next:

Coffee. Chocolate.

It was heady and intoxicating.

I stumbled toward the break room, heart hammering.

Zeff staggered out, one hand gripping the wall, the other pressed flat against his thigh like he was trying to ground himself. His jaw was clenched, teeth gritted against a low, guttural sound rising in his chest.

"Zeff?" My voice cracked, heat spiking in my core.

He dropped to his knees halfway down the bathroom hall, panting. One hand braced against the floor, the other clawed at the wall like he was holding himself together.

Then I saw it.

His shirt stretched, seams tugging. His body looked… different. Bigger. It felt as if something beneath his skin was trying to break free. Heat shimmered around him in waves, the air warping like it does above asphalt on a summer day.

I couldn't breathe.

My senses drowned in him—his scent, his energy, and his need. It pulled at something deep and animalistic inside me.

Then his head jerked up, and our eyes met.

The familiar green has vanished. Two pitch-black, famished eyes gazed back, full of hunger.

"Don't come closer," he gasped. "I—I can't hold it back—"

But I was already moving. The heat clawing my skin was pulling me over to him like gravity. "What's going on? Why are you in pain?"

"I'm not in pain," he growled, his voice ragged. He stood—slowly, deliberately—and every inch of his body seemed to pulse with power. The scent around him was intoxicating now, more than I could bear. His shirt ripped slightly at the collar as his shoulders broadened. "I'm in need."

That word hit me harder than it should have. I stopped a foot away from him, trembling. His pupils dilated, and I could see his entire body straining against the clothing. My breath caught when I noticed him. Hard. Visibly hard.

The sight sent a wave of liquid heat straight to my core, and suddenly, the ache in my chest became unbearable. I needed to touch him. To feel him. My body wasn't just craving—it was begging. He took a step back, approaching the restroom as if it were the solution.

"What do I do?" I asked, my voice trembling too. "Zeff—tell me what to do."

He looked at me like he wanted to devour me. His back rested against the end wall of the hallway just beside the men's bathroom door.

"Leave."

I should have run.

I didn't. Instead, I took a step closer, like a gravitational pull.

He exhaled sharply, his control fraying. "Liliam… Please."

Zeff's eyes locked onto me, black and hungry. They dragged down my body like a physical caress—from my parted lips to the curve of my waist and lower still, settling between my thighs. Every place his gaze touched flared to life, heat blooming beneath my skin like fire licking along dry kindling. "I don't want to do something you'll regret."

I closed my eyes and breathed in, and it was ten times worse. My entire body was screaming to feel him, to kiss him, and to touch him.

I moved. Or maybe he did.

All I knew was when my body pressed on his chest, his mouth crashed onto mine, and everything else ceased to exist. The world narrowed to the sensations of heat and lips, along with the rapid rasp of shared breath. My back slammed into the wall with a gasp, and his arms were already around me—one tangled in my hair, the other sliding down my thigh as he lifted me effortlessly. My legs wrapped around him on instinct, dragging him tighter against me.

The hardness between us pressed right where I needed it, and I gasped against his mouth.

His kiss wasn't sweet. It was consuming. A claim. A confession of everything he hadn't said. His tongue thrusts deep, tasting, devouring. Every moan I gave was swallowed whole, every desperate noise turned to fuel for the fire raging between us.

"You have no idea," he growled, his voice frayed with need, "how hard I've fought this. How long I've wanted to feel you."

I couldn't speak. I could barely think. There was only this sensation.

His hands slid beneath my shirt, rough palms meeting bare skin. I arched into the touch, my spine bowing as he mapped every inch of me—up my ribs, down my back, fingers skating so close to my breasts I whimpered.

His mouth trailed lower, finding my throat. He kissed and then licked the spot just beneath my ear, sending shudders through my entire body. When he bit down—just enough to sting—I cried out, my fingers tangling in his hair.

"Zeff," I panted, writhing against him. "This is… insane."

"Then tell me to stop," he rasped, dragging his lips across my jaw, back to my mouth. "Tell me, Liliam."

But I didn't. I couldn't.

Everything within me was urging me to say yes—yes to his hands, his mouth, and his body nestled between my thighs. Yes, to this heat that had been building for far too long.

So instead of answering, I pulled him closer and kissed him like I was drowning.

And he kissed me back like I was the air he'd been denied for far too long.

****

Zeff

I was gone.

There was no more thinking—no reason, no control.

Just her.

Josh had warned me about the Parr. We knew it was close. I didn't know if I was too worn out to calculate correctly or notice the signs, but I was sure I had a week before it. It would have been my first Parr finding my mate.

I feared what it would be like knowing my mate was nearby. But Goddess, I didn't expect the Parr to strike while I was standing just a few feet away from her.

And fucking Goddess. My years of control went out the window.

The moment we kissed, Liliam burned in my arms—her lips parting beneath mine like they'd been waiting for this, for me. Her moans, the drag of her nails down my back, the way her legs locked around my hips—everything blurred into one consuming need. Relentless. Addictive. The Parr had snapped through my veins like a whip. Every cell inside me howled to take her, to bind her, to make her mine.

"My whole body," she gasped, trembling, "it's on fire."

I knew. The bond was opening. She was experiencing the same emotions as me, engulfed by the tempest I could barely control. And fuck, I felt guilty—for tangling her in something so ancient, so consuming.

"You don't understand what this feeling does to me," I rasped, my voice raw. "How hard it is to hold back."

But her mouth met mine again, desperate and wild. My hands gripped her hips, dragging her closer until there was nothing left between us but breath—and destiny.

I lifted her effortlessly and carried her into the men's bathroom, a small mercy of privacy from the office cameras. I wasn't about to put her at risk—not like that.

Setting her down on the vanity, I cursed the heat, the ache, and the need that wouldn't let me go. It wasn't the setting I wanted for her… But I was already past the point of return.

"Tell me," I said, voice barely human, "tell me you want this."

Her cheeks were flushed, eyes wide, and pupils dilated with desire. She moaned, fingers locking behind my neck, pulling me closer.

"I need you," she whispered.

Those three words undid me.

I kissed her again—deeper, fiercer—and this time, there was no stopping. My hand pushed up her skirt, sliding up her thighs. She moaned into my mouth, hips lifting in invitation.

I felt the heat of her core as my fingers brushed her, wet and trembling beneath my touch.

She broke the kiss, head falling back against the mirror, lips parted in a breathless gasp.

Goddess. She was ready. Slick. Wanting.

My cock pulsed in response, hard and aching.

I fumbled with the buttons of my pants, yanking down my waistband just enough to free myself. One desperate motion—one breathless heartbeat—and I slid into her.

She shattered.

Pleasure slammed through me like lightning—raw, blinding. The fire ignited between us, no longer simmering but blazing. Every thrust, every gasp, every scrape of skin was a vow—ancient and unspoken.

Etched into our bones.

We moved as if destined to be together. No hesitation. No shame. Only need. Only us.

She clung to me, holding on like I was the only thing anchoring her to this world.

Our bodies moved together in rhythm—breath to breath, skin to skin—each thrust drawing us closer to the edge. Her cries, her scent, and her heat—they drove me insane. I was unraveling inside her.

"Zeff," she moaned—my name breaking on her lips like a prayer.

That sound… it was sacred. And it was mine.

My pace faltered—hips jerking harder, deeper—pressure building until I thought I'd explode.

"Don't stop," she begged, desperate, trembling. "Please…"

And I didn't.

I drove deeper, chasing the moment. We were on the verge of a moment where our souls would unite and cease to resist our inherent essence.

When it came—when she cried out, clenching around me with a silent scream—I followed. My body seized, vision white-hot, the Parr detonating through me in a wave of pure, devastating release.

I collapsed against her, forehead to forehead, panting through the haze. My chest heaved, my heartbeat still pounding like war drums. Every part of me shook—from the force, from the bond, from the way her body had taken me in like a prayer.

And hers… trembled beneath mine.

Her fingers unclenched from my shoulders. Her legs slowly slipped from around my waist.

And then—she stilled.

The heat didn't vanish. No, it twisted. It curled sharply and coldly beneath my skin, like a blade pressed too deep.

I opened my eyes, and I saw it.

The guilt.

Her eyes shimmered, her lips parted, and her breath came in broken gasps. Her skin flushed, pupils still blown wide. But her expression…?

It was an open wound.

Like she'd just broken something sacred.

"Liliam," I murmured, brushing my knuckles gently along her jaw. My voice cracked. "Are you okay?"

She flinched.

My touch seemed to burn her now.

Her body jerked upright—like she'd just woken from a dream that had turned, suddenly, into a nightmare.

"I—I need to go." Her voice sounded clipped. Hollow. Already retreating behind walls, I couldn't scale.

"No—wait." I quickly buttoned my pants and took a step back. "Please just let me explain—this isn't—"

But she was already off the vanity, already covering herself, clothes half-on, not looking at me. Not once.

She avoided my gaze as if I were the flame she desperately sought to flee.

"Liliam," I breathed, feeling desperate as I followed her, my body still humming with the echo of her presence and my blood singing her name.

She bolted.

The door slammed shut behind her.

And I stood there trembling and drenched in sweat. The air is still thick with the scent of us. The Parr is still surging through my veins like lightning with nowhere to strike.

But the room? Silent.

And it was colder than it had any right to be.

Gaius, my wolf, paced beneath my skin—restless. Snarling. Agitated.

We had her.

And you didn't mark her.

I stumbled back, bracing one hand against the wall as the ache hit—hard. Physical. It felt as if a part of me had been ripped out along with her.

I could still smell her. Still taste her.

I still feel the imprint of her thighs clamped around my waist, her lips trembling against mine.

I sank to the floor. A ragged breath left me.

I buried one hand in my hair. The other hand was fisted against the cold tile as I tried not to punch straight through it.

She ran. She ran, not because she didn't desire it.

She ran because her desire for it was overwhelming.

And that terrified her.

****

Colorado, US

The taste of stale whiskey clung to my tongue like rot as my silver eyes cracked open against the merciless glare of morning. Light speared through the slats in the heavy curtains, stabbing straight into my skull. Pain bloomed behind my temples, rhythmic and brutal—each throb a cruel reminder of the night before.

I groaned, dragging a hand over my face, half-praying for darkness to take me again.

It didn't. Instead, I felt warmth. Breathe. I noticed a slight change in the sheets next to me.

I turned my head—and there she was.

The little maid. She was barely more than a girl, with long brown hair that was braided neatly down her back and now fanned across my pillow like spilled molasses. Her skin, pale and porcelain-fine, was marred—faint bruises blooming along her collarbone, bite marks trailing down her throat to her shoulder. Red and raw.

Memories unraveled in disjointed flashes. Her eyes lowered every time I passed her in the corridor. Her hands trembled noticeably as she handed me my coffee. She had flushed crimson when I brushed my fingers against her wrist. Her lips parted in breathless submission as I took what I wanted

And she had given it. All of it. No protest. Only soft sounds and clumsy knees were audible.

She stirred, her lashes fluttering. Blue eyes—wide, frightened—met mine. Her whole body went still as reality crashed into her.

"I'm sorry, Your Majesty," she whispered, her voice thin, broken around shame.

I didn't answer with words. I waved a hand lazily, my voice a low rasp of disinterest. "Get treated. Then leave."

She scrambled out of the bed like a cornered deer, clutching the blanket to her chest as she fled. The scent of fear lingered after her, mingling with blood and sweat and guilt.

I sat up slowly, every movement sending shards of pain through my skull. The room was a wreck. The sheets twisted, the air thick with the remnants of heat and alcohol. I reached for the half-empty glass of water on the nightstand, but before it touched my lips, the door creaked open.

Elias. My Beta. He wasn't just my beta—he was the son of my father's old friend, a remnant of the pack that had raised me. When I rose to claim the throne, he and a handful of loyal wolves had abandoned Montana's broken foster-home packs to follow me to Colorado.

He stepped in with the quiet precision of a soldier, his brown eyes scanning the carnage—disheveled bed, fading footsteps, and me, half-naked and barely holding onto patience. He sighed, tucking the wavy strands of brown hair at the back of his ear; the sound was heavy with judgment he didn't voice. "Your Majesty," he said carefully.

I rubbed my face again and didn't bother masking my irritation. "Spare me the sermon, Elias." I said I'm already tired of this conversation.

"You shouldn't have done that," Elias said, his voice even. "The Council is already watching you closely. They won't like you bedding the staff."

"Not your fucking concern," I snapped, my voice low and cutting. It sliced through the air like frost, and the room stilled around it.

But Elias, loyal bastard that he was, didn't even blink. He never did. Not when I shattered ribs. Not when I razed rebel dens to ash. Not when I made enemies beg for death.

I pushed to my feet, stalking to the full-length mirror near the bathroom. My sandy hair was a mess, tangled and matted. Red marks lined my abdomen—her nails, probably. She'd liked it. They always did. I was a god to them. Beautiful. Untouchable. Brutal.

"What," I growled, locking eyes with my reflection, "brought you here to ruin my hangover?"

Elias shifted, hesitation flickering across his usually unreadable face. "Word from Montana. Gunnolf… he found his mate."

The rage was immediate. A firestorm ignited in my chest, quickly devouring the fog of alcohol.

"And?" I hissed.

"The Council's talking. The Council is discussing the stability it brings to their territory. About the power of the bond. They're—"

He didn't finish. He didn't need to.

They were already comparing us. Again.

How I, King of Kings, still walked alone.

How I still hadn't found my Luna.

How I was now the unstable one in their fucking ledger.

The lamp on the nightstand exploded under my hand, glass flying as it shattered against the stone wall.

Elias remained motionless. Of course he did.

"I won the challenge," I said through clenched teeth. "I earned the crown. I broke every wolf they sent. And now they're pissing themselves over Gunnolf because he happened to find someone to share his fucking bed?" Silence stretched between us.

Elias waited.

Slowly, the fury simmered down into something worse: cold calculation.

My lip curled into a slow, dangerous smile.

"Prepare an escort," I said, my voice calm now. Deadly calm. "We're going to Montana."

Elias hesitated just a fraction too long.

I turned my gaze on him, letting him feel the full weight of it.

"Now."

He bowed low. "As you command, Your Majesty."

The door shut behind him.

I stood alone in the wreckage, blood humming beneath my skin. My fists flexed, nails biting into my palm.

If Gunnolf thought fate had smiled on him, he hadn't yet seen what a king does when backed into a corner.

Let him have his little miracle.

I was coming for it.

12
SINISTER

Liliam

I didn't sleep.

Not really.

I lay in bed with the sheets twisted around my legs, the scent of Shadow's fur a small comfort at my feet, but even his warmth couldn't quiet the storm inside me.

Every time I closed my eyes, I felt Zeff's hands again. The heat of his palms splayed across my skin. The way he had growled my name like it belonged to him.

And God help me—I had answered.

I'd wrapped myself around him, kissed him like I was starved, and begged with my body for more until there was nothing between us but breath and fire. And when he moved inside me, when our bodies collided like a storm cracking the sky—I hadn't stopped him.

I hadn't wanted to stop him.

And the worst part?

I wanted it again. I wanted him.

The memory alone made my body ache. My thighs trembled when I moved. I could still feel the ghost of his touch between my legs. My lips were swollen and bitten.

And yet it was my heart that hurt most.

My chest continued to tighten as I sat alone in my room, wrapped in a blanket.

What had I done?

I curled my knees to my chest, burying my face in them, but it didn't help. I could still feel him. He whispered my name, his breath at my neck, his voice rough and broken.

I shouldn't have allowed it to occur.

I had a boyfriend.

My life was filled with plans.

But with Zeff… none of it made sense anymore. Logic was no longer relevant in this situation. The situation wasn't about timing or morals or any of the things I'd clung to for comfort.

This affair was something else.

I'd kissed Zeff back with everything I had. I'd pulled him into me like I couldn't breathe without him. There was no denying what it was anymore—not a crush, not curiosity.

The need for him was overwhelming.

Raw. Electric. Terrifying.

It wasn't just that he saw me—it was that when he touched me, it felt like something inside me woke up. He was the only one who ever bothered to wake me up, even though I'd spent my entire life half-asleep.

And now?

Now I didn't know how to go back.

Too normal. To Owen. To the version of me that hadn't been unraveled and rewired by the hands of a man who might not even be human.

Zeff's gaze on me afterward was not merely possessive.

It was primal. Raw instinct. Animal instinct.

And now I couldn't stop replaying what I saw—what I felt.

The darkening of his forearms and the way his skin rippled with shadowed fur captivated me. Claws, not nails, had gripped my thighs. He had fangs that gleamed faintly, longer than any human should possess. I'd felt them. The fangs were pressed against my tongue. Against my skin.

What's even more terrifying?

I hadn't pulled away. I had craved it.

And now I was starting to wonder if I had been wrong about everything—

About Zeff.

The events that transpired in that office weren't solely driven by desire.

It was something deeper. Wilder. It felt as though a force had established itself beneath my skin, pulling me down.

And I couldn't control it. I always controlled it. Desire never ruled me.

Until him.

His touch rewrote every law I lived by. It wasn't just heat. It was fantasy.

I had read about it in books and never thought it could be real.

My alarm buzzed at 5:30, sharp and cruel.

Shadow lifted his head from my ankle with a little huff, blinking at me as if to say, "You good?"

"No," I whispered, dragging my hand over my face. "Not even close."

My chest felt like barbed wire by the time I dressed and headed out the door.

The ride to work passed in a blur of pavement and static silence. Owen didn't speak—not that I expected him to. Our silences had teeth now. The words were sharp and deliberate, containing all the things we didn't say and perhaps never would.

But the moment I walked into the office, the air shifted— and my stomach dropped.

Zeff was already there.

Zeff was already standing by the copy machine.

Fresh shirt. Sleeves rolled to the elbow. His hair was damp, like he'd just stepped out of the shower, steam still clinging to his skin. And somehow—infuriatingly, unfairly—he looked like something carved out of temptation itself.

My body reacted before my brain did.

Heat surged across my skin like a flash fire. Every nerve lit up like it remembered his hands, his mouth, and his weight against me. I could still feel where he'd touched me, where he'd been inside me. My pulse skittered.

He looked up at the sound of the door—and God help me, his eyes locked on mine like they'd been waiting.

For a second—just one second—his expression shifted. Hunger. Tension. Restraint. Then it vanished, buried beneath the cool, unreadable calm he wore like armor.

He turned back to the copy machine like nothing had happened.

He acted as though I hadn't run out on him, my legs trembling and my soul ablaze.

Like we didn't—

Fuck in the bathroom.

I swallowed hard, the taste of him still ghosting my tongue. I forced myself past him, every step a war against my body. His scent hit me—coffee and heat—and my knees nearly buckled.

I barely made it to my desk before collapsing into my chair, hands trembling, chest tight.

Get it together, Liliam.

I opened my laptop, pretending to work, pretending to breathe—but all I could feel was him.

I could feel every shift in his weight.

He was whispering to someone across the room. He assumed that I wouldn't notice every glance he cast.

But I did.

And when I finally met his gaze—fully, unflinching—something in me twisted.

Because he didn't look frustrated or smug or regretful.

He looked… patient.

He appeared as though he was patiently awaiting my decision.

He was patiently waiting for me to decide.

To speak. To move. To run—or not.

And I didn't know what terrified me more: that I might run again… Or that this time, I wouldn't.

****

The office emptied slowly, one voice at a time, leaving behind nothing but the low hum of overhead lights and the stale scent of takeout containers. I stood near the front desk, phone pressed to my ear, listening to Owen's voicemail message for the fourth time.

There was still no response. Of course.

I let my arm drop to my side and stared through the glass doors into the parking lot beyond. Night had fallen completely. The asphalt shimmered under the yellowed glow of the streetlamp, but not a single car was in sight. My rideshare app blinked uselessly—glitching between "searching" and a frozen loading screen that felt like the universe's cruelest joke.

"Are you okay?"

Zeff's voice was behind me. I didn't turn around. I didn't want him to see how troubled I was. "Owen's not answering. Apps frozen. I guess I'm just… here."

"I'll take you."

That made me turn. He stood a few feet away, hands in his jacket pockets, expression unreadable but eyes steady on mine.

"I would rather not be a problem," I said, a little too softly.

"You're not." His voice was firmer this time. "Come on. I already texted my friend Josh."

I hesitated. My body didn't. I followed him out into the parking lot, our steps echoing across the empty pavement. A part of me screamed to retreat. It wasn't that I didn't desire to be close to him, but rather, I craved it.

Too much.

I couldn't escape the memory of his mouth, his hands, and the way he had looked at me like I was the only thing anchoring him to this world. The night still carried a faint scent of him. Not when I could feel my skin pulse with phantom heat.

A low rumble cut through my thoughts. A sleek black truck rolled to a stop beside the curb, its engine purring like something alive.

The window rolled down.

The man behind the wheel was large, broad across the shoulders, with a clean-cut jaw and dark eyes that flicked to me the moment I approached. His posture was sharp and controlled. But when our eyes met—

He stiffened.

His head dipped—once. He made a bow without turning his head.

"Luna," he said, low and reverent.

I blinked. "What—?"

"This is Josh," Zeff said quickly, stepping beside me. His tone was calm, but I saw the flick of his fingers—a small, silent correction.

Josh immediately adjusted. He looked at Zeff and looked away.

It was subtle. But not lost on me.

"Thanks for the ride," I murmured, awkwardly, as I slipped into the passenger seat. Zeff climbed into the back.

Josh simply nodded. "Of course."

The drive was quiet—only the roaring engine of the truck and the cars passing by.

Josh glanced at me, but it seemed as if he was trying not to stare directly at the sun.

I didn't know what to do with that.

When we pulled up to the house, Shadow was already waiting at the door. I'd had a small pet door installed for him not long ago, but he rarely used it to wander. He never strayed far—always followed me, leash or not, like a silent shadow bound to my steps.

His little body stood still, ears perked, head lifted high. Eyes locked on the truck before it had even finished rolling to a stop.

Watching. Waiting.

I stepped out and braced myself for his usual greeting—tail wagging, paws against my knees, joyful howls.

But he didn't run. He didn't even bark.

Then, slowly—deliberately—he lowered his head like a bow. His ears flattened. He looked like he was kneeling.

"Shadow?" I whispered, stunned. He didn't look at me.

Zeff stepped out behind me, the gravel crunching beneath his boots. Shadow remained where he was, unmoving.

When Zeff stood beside me, I could feel this aura emanating from him. I experienced a strong, commanding sensation.

"Come," Zeff said. The word was "low." Gentle.

Shadow obeyed instantly, rising and moving toward Zeff with his head still lowered. He stopped in front of him, pressing his nose to his leg.

I couldn't breathe.

Zeff crouched, running his hand over Shadow's head once, like a king knighting a soldier. Josh watched, as still as stone; when he met my gaze, he immediately looked down at the floor, then turned and slipped into the driver's seat without saying a word.

And then—Zeff stilled.

A shift occurred in the atmosphere. I felt it too, a sudden weight in my chest. The temperature didn't drop, but it felt like it had. The quiet wasn't peaceful anymore. It was watched.

Zeff's posture straightened, his shoulders rising with a slow inhale. His eyes scanned the tree line like he was hearing something I couldn't, his jaw clenching ever so slightly.

His whole energy shifted. The Zeff I knew in the office had vanished. This Zeff was something else. Alert. On edge. There was a shadow that seemed poised to move.

I stood on the porch, arms crossed tightly around my chest, voice barely a breath. "Zeff… what just happened?"

He turned slowly. His hand still rested on Shadow's back, but his eyes had darkened—not with desire. With focus.

"Something's close."

"Close?" I echoed, confused and afraid.

"I don't like the way the air smells." He glanced at the woods beyond the house. "Go inside. Lock the door."

"Zeff—"

"Now, Liliam," he said again, this time sharper, eyes not on me anymore but on the shadows of the tree.

"Shadow, go as well."

As I stepped inside, locking the door behind me, I took one last look back through the glass.

Zeff hadn't moved.

But his eyes…

His green eyes were glowing.

****

The door clicked shut behind me, and I turned the lock. Twice.

I leaned against it, forehead pressing to the wood, trying to quiet my pulse—loud, frantic, like the beat of a trapped bird's wings.

Zeff's voice still echoed in my ears. "Go inside. Lock the door."

The thought slithered down my spine. I turned slowly, the room around me dim and still. The glow from the lamp barely touched the corners. It felt like the house was holding its breath.

Shadow trotted quietly through the small dog door. Watchful. He sat beside me on the couch—not nuzzling, not yipping—just sitting and staring at the door.

As if waiting for more instructions

I brushed my fingers through his fur, my hand shaking slightly. "You're not acting like yourself," I whispered.

But then again… Neither was I.

Because every time I closed my eyes, I could still feel Zeff.

The heat of him. The weight of his body pressing mine into the wall. The way I had opened to him—like I had been starving and didn't know it until he touched me.

The moment his mouth claimed mine, I never stood a chance as the heat surged between us and the world narrowed to just our breath.

I had wrapped my legs around him without thinking.

Let him in completely. Mind. Body. Soul.

And now?

Now I couldn't breathe without remembering it.

His scent still clung to my skin. Faint and wild. Every shift on the couch dragged a ghost of the memory back—between my thighs, in the dull ache I tried to ignore, in the phantom press of his lips on my neck.

My thoughts spun like a storm. Tangled emotions, feelings I couldn't define, and a reality I wasn't sure I could trust anymore.

What the hell was happening to me?

My laptop sat open on the table—an anchor to logic, to something familiar. I reached for it like it could save me.

Just a little research, I told myself. *Just something to clear my head.*

But deep down, I knew.

The similarities between those damn fantasy books and what was happening to me weren't just coincidence anymore.

I just needed the words. I needed something tangible to solidify the situation. I typed slowly:

"Wolf bond signs"

The results poured in—articles, forums, and excerpts from romance books that I would've laughed at weeks ago.

Now?

They read like confessions.

I clicked a wiki entry titled "The Luna Bond."

"A Luna is the fated mate of the Alpha. Her presence calms the beast. Her scent triggers the bond. Once claimed, the bond becomes physical, spiritual—unbreakable. The alpha will become territorial, possessive, and biologically unable to desire another." My throat tightened.

I swallowed hard.

Another link.

"Wolves have a mating season. During this time, the heat of reproduction and bonding overwhelms them. Instinct dominates. Most mates experience it as intense heat, primal craving, and emotional fusion. They may also exhibit supernatural sensitivity—dreams, heightened physical responses, and even changes in behavior from nearby animals."

I blinked.

Well. Shit.

A wave of heat flushed through my chest, blooming low and deep.

I shifted in my seat. My thighs pressed together tightly, trying—and failing—to suppress the memory that clawed its way up my spine.

His mouth. His hands. His body was positioned over mine, wrapped around me, and inside me.

The way he had pinned me to that vanity like I was something sacred and untouchable—and ruined me in the same breath.

How I had begged—genuinely begged—for more. He needs to keep going.

For him to never stop.

And when we both came—gods, it hadn't just been sex.

It felt like something ancient had cracked open inside me and poured through every nerve.

It felt like belonging.

I slammed the laptop shut, my breath catching.

Too much. Too real.

I sat there, frozen, heart thundering in my chest. My fingers trembled in my lap. My whole body still hummed with phantom sensation.

I wanted so badly to believe this was all just fantasy. I believed that Zeff was merely a man—a dangerously attractive man with a rough voice and an air of mystery.

And me? Just a woman caught in the unraveling threads of a failing relationship.

Desperate. Confused. Vulnerable.

But I knew better. I had more than just a desire for him the previous night. I'd needed him. In a way I couldn't explain. In a way, that rewrote something in me.

And now, I wasn't sure who I was without him. His touch lingered in places that no one else had ever reached. Because when he told me to lock the door, I had.

Not out of fear. But because somewhere deep inside me, a voice I didn't recognize whispered,

He's not done with you.

My gaze flicked toward Shadow.

The little wolf pup sat at the threshold, watching the door like a sentry—eyes sharp, posture tense, ears alert.

Like he was waiting for someone. Or guarding someone. Me?

My mind spun in dizzy circles, toeing the edge between reason and delusion.

Is my brain just connecting dots that aren't there? Or is this the beginning of something I can't take back?

****

Owen

I was trying my best to keep it together.

Seeing Liliam spending time with that goddamn idiot—Zeff—who always smelled like smoke, sweat, and something primal I couldn't name, was taking a toll on me. Every time I saw her near him, smiling, laughing, leaning just a little too close, it felt like someone was tightening a noose around my ribs.

I know what I did a year ago. I was drunk—so far gone I woke up tangled in sheets that weren't hers, with a girl whose name I don't even remember. It was reckless. Pathetic. And I'd give anything to take it back.

Liliam didn't deserve that.

But I loved her. I told her the truth. I told her it was a mistake—that it would never happen again.

And it hasn't.

But things between us haven't been the same since. The connection we used to have—the effortless laughter, the quiet understanding, the way she used to look at me like I was her whole world—it's fractured.

I've been trying to rebuild it. Brick by goddamn brick. And she's tried too. I see it in the way she smiles at me occasionally. But I also see when that smile falters, when her eyes dim, and she slips on her headphones to drown out the silence between us.

That's the sign. The one that guts me. She's still struggling. Still doubting.

And yet—I've stayed. I've kept my hands to myself. I've held back every frustrated urge, every jealous snap, and every desire because I want to be better. For her.

But God... The tension's burning through my veins. What's the most distressing aspect?

I'm aware that a new man has entered the picture. Bigger. Stronger. Always there. Always hovering.

And she laughs with him.

Laughs.

I haven't heard that sound from her in months.

And it pisses me off more than I want to admit. Not because I don't trust her—but because deep down, I know she's slipping through my fingers.

And I'm terrified I've already lost her.

At work, I did my best to block out the constant hum of gossip. But fuck—if you're hoping for a drama-free environment, the office isn't it. People thrive on chaos. They feed on whispers, on half-truths, on stories twisted just enough to sting.

And lately, those whispers had a name.

Liliam.

I could feel the eyes on me—behind my back, across the room—watching, waiting, lips mouthing her name like it was some dirty secret. It felt as if I was already drowning in guilt while trying to keep my composure.

It was exhausting.

Therefore, when my manager offered me an off-site installation gig, I took it without hesitation. No questions. No complaints.

Anything to get the hell out of that building.

The new client required a high-end security package. I'd done the task a dozen times before—usually for government offices, high-profile lawyers, and sometimes private labs. However, this particular client felt off the moment I stepped inside.

The space was too quiet. The lights dimmed low, creating a sense of isolation from the rest of the building. One male receptionist greeted me with a blank expression. But there was no tech team nor security. Just one man was waiting in the center of the conference room, leaning back in a leather chair like he owned me.

He stood as I entered, his smile too wide. Too warm.

"Good afternoon, Mr. Greene," he said, extending a hand. Smooth. Too smooth. Skin as cold as polished stone.

I gripped his hand out of reflex, and a chill seeped into my bones. "Of course," I replied evenly, suppressing the instinctive shiver. "I handle our elite clients personally."

We got to work. Or—at least, I tried.

Every time I pulled up schematics or reviewed the system specifications, I could feel his gaze on me.

Like he already knew every inch of me—and was just savoring the confirmation. He didn't ask about the equipment's specs. He didn't even glance at the designs.

No—he asked about me.

"You served in the Marines, didn't you?" He asked, his voice casual, almost bored, like we were two old friends catching up.

I stiffened, hiding it beneath a controlled breath. Few people knew about those years. Even fewer had the clearance to find out. Unless…

"Honorable discharge," I said tightly. "Four years," I narrowed my eyes. "How do you know this?"

He smiled again—too slow, too knowing—and tapped a pen lightly against the desk.

Tap. Tap. Tap.

"Strong. Disciplined. Broken in… but still functional."

My pulse kicked harder. "What did you just say?" I asked, my voice low.

He leaned forward, elbows on the desk, voice dropping into a whisper.

"Knowing yourself is important. Especially when you've spent so long pretending to be something you're not."

Something deep in my gut twisted. That tight-coiled spring that every soldier knows—the one that means danger. Now.

I blinked. I felt a surge of heat behind my eyes.

He continued smoothly, saying, "When I read your file, I was surprised." This corporal took down 23 targets in a single operation. Then promoted to the Raiders. That is outright uncommon. To see so many blacked-out lines." He smiled wider, eyes gleaming. "Those were my favorite."

I stared him down, blood thundering in my ears. "What the hell are you getting at?"

He didn't answer.

Instead—almost tenderly—he asked, "How's Liliam doing?"

The air left my lungs in a rush. My spine locked rigid.

He chuckled—low and amused, like I'd just said something adorable. "Oh, Owen… everyone important knows about Liliam." He tilted his head. "The bright little moon that made a ghost think he could be human again."

A beat of silence. I took a step back, fists clenching. My instincts were screaming now—run, fight, kill.

"Who the hell are you?" I demanded.

His smile turned razor-sharp. "Someone reminding you what you really are."

Before I could move, before I could react—

The lights above flickered.

A pressure, similar to that of a giant's hand, crushed my skull.

My vision snapped from white—

to black—to red.

The room pulsed like a living thing. My heart slammed against my ribs, my body jerking with the effort to stay standing.

I staggered, reaching for something—anything—

Then the floor heaved beneath me. My knees buckled.

And I fell into darkness.

****

Seven Years Ago

The room smelled like sweat, dust, and steel. Cold and stale, the room smelled like military bases do after too many years of pretending honor still mattered.

I sat stiff in the metal chair, hands resting lightly on my thighs, blood still drying under my nails.

Across the room, Colonel Anders walked in, slow and deliberate, as if he already understood my response before posing the question. He was tall and lean, his perfectly pressed uniform.

His face was all sharp lines: a squared jaw, hawk-like nose, and piercing gray eyes that seemed to weigh and measure every weakness in a man within seconds.

His close-cropped hair was more iron than silver, and his mouth rarely formed anything but a thin, assessing line—like even breathing was a calculation.

There wasn't a hint of kindness in him.

Only precision. Only purpose.

He didn't speak at first. I just pressed a button on the projector.

The screen came alive in shades of green and gray.

The screen displayed grainy footage of night vision. I recognized it instantly—the last mission. No one else had successfully completed the mission.

My squad. The compound. Silence engulfed the screams.

Colonel Anders moved beside the screen, hands clasped neatly behind his back, voice low and clinical:

"You moved like a ghost," he said.

The footage showed me breaching a door, gun in one hand, knife in the other—brutal, fast, silent. Enemies fell without a sound, each takedown more efficient than the last.

I didn't blink as I watched it. But I felt the hum stir again beneath my skin. That other thing. A part of me stood by their side, recalling the sensation of their presence.

"Twenty-three hostiles," Anders continued, his tone almost bored. "Neutralized."

The scene shifted—me dragging an enemy into the shadows, slicing a throat cleanly, the body dropping without a sound.

"Guns. Knives. Bare hands."

Another cut: I weaved through gunfire like I could see the bullets coming—every shot I fired hit its mark.

Head. Chest. Throat. No hesitation. There was no second-guessing. This was the part they would have watched on loop. A man—one of the enemy soldiers—threw down his rifle, raised his hands, and pleaded in a language I didn't understand.

I remembered it perfectly. How did I hesitate?

The pause lasted for half a second. The footage zoomed in. For just that instant, one of my eyes glowed faint red in the night vision.

A flicker.

A pulse.

A monster emerges from beneath a man's skin.

Then, without flinching, I pulled the trigger. The man collapsed.

The screen froze there—the flash of the muzzle lighting up my blank face, the eerie glint of red in my right eye, like something monstrous staring out from behind my skin.

Colonel Anders let the image hang in the air before killing the projector. He turned, moving closer, his boots slow against the concrete floor like a ticking clock.

"You fought like a man with nothing to lose," he said.

I didn't respond. What was there to say? He wasn't wrong.

"And we need men like that," he said, his voice almost gentle—but it was a hunter's gentleness, the kind that lured prey closer before snapping the trap shut.

He circled me—slow, measured—like a vulture deciding which part to carve first.

"We're offering you something no one else will," he continued. "A place where men like you don't have to pretend."

My jaw tightened. Pretend to be human. Pretend to care. Assume the rules apply to me just as they do to everyone else.

I kept my voice low and detached. "And if I say no?"

Colonel Anders smiled—but there was nothing warm about it. It was the kind of smile you give a dog you're about to leash or put down.

"Then we bury you under medals and paperwork," he said. "Make you a decorated ghost. Pretend we don't see what you really are."

He leaned closer, the overhead light carving deep shadows into the lines of his face.

"But if you say yes…" His voice dropped lower, hungrier. "You'll be more than a soldier."

The silence that followed stretched like taut wire.

I lifted my head slowly, letting him see the thing he was talking to—the part of me that didn't flinch, didn't bleed inside anymore. Dead calm. Calculating.

My mouth barely moved.

"When do I start?"

The faintest smile pulled at Anders' lips—not pleased, not proud. Just satisfied.

He slid a thick black dossier across the table toward me.

The folder was unmarked except for a single symbol—a dark snake head burned into the cover.

No rules. No borders. No conscience.

I signed my name without hesitation.

****

Present

I regained consciousness while lying on the cold tile floor. My palms were slick—wet.

I blinked hard. The overhead lights flickered back to life, illuminating the horror around me.

Blood was everywhere.

Blood was spattered across the walls and pooled beneath the conference table. It dripped from the corners of the windows. My hands—my hands—were soaked in it. Thick. Tacky. Still warm.

And the bodies—

There were three of them.

The bodies appeared to be those of security personnel. Ripped open. Throats torn. One man's skull was crushed like a tin can. I recognized his ID badge. I'd spoken to him on the way in.

My breath caught. A scream built in my throat, but no sound came out.

He had vanished. There was no sign of his presence. Not even a footprint.

Just the blood. And there was a single, perfectly pressed card left on the table, untouched by the carnage:

A monster will always be a monster.

I stumbled back, nearly slipping in the blood pooled around my boots.

The bodies. The blood.

My heart slammed against my ribs like it was trying to break free from my chest. My stomach lurched, bile rising in my throat, but I forced it down. I couldn't throw up.

Think, Owen. Think.

But my mind—my own fucking mind—was cracked wide open. There were flashes I didn't understand. Claws. Growls. My hands are ripping. My mouth is biting.

No. That wasn't me.

That couldn't be me.

I clutched the edge of the table, breathing hard, trying to steady myself. "This isn't real," I muttered under my breath. "I didn't do this. I couldn't have done this."

But the red dripping from my fingertips said otherwise.

The door was open. I don't remember opening it.

My body moved on instinct, dragging me out of the carnage and into the corridor. Down the emergency stairs. Out the back entrance.

Cold air hit me like a slap. I leaned against the alley wall, gulping down breath after breath.

Liliam.

I remember the exact moment I met her. It was just after one of my last field raids—my gear still smelled like sweat and sand, the weight of everything I'd seen clinging to me like a second skin. I had stopped by McAllen University to hand over some classified reports to Colonel Marshall, who was hosting a recruiting event. The halls were buzzing with life—students laughing, rushing, unaware of the darker parts of the world that waited beyond the campus gates.

And then—her.

I turned a corner too fast, not looking where I was going, and we collided. Hard.

Her textbooks hit the floor with a loud smack, pages splaying everywhere. A drawing pad tumbled last, sliding just far enough for me to catch a glimpse of it. Charcoal sketches. Delicate hands. The eyes in the sketches conveyed too much emotion to be merely lines on a page.

"Shit—sorry," I muttered, already bending to help her.

Then she looked up.

And the world… stopped.

It felt as if someone had struck me in the chest or jolted me straight to the heart. Her eyes—deep, amber, framed by lashes too long to be real—locked onto mine, and I swear I forgot my name. Her hair spilled around her shoulders in soft waves, and her lips parted, caught somewhere between surprise and amusement.

"Are you okay?" I asked, but my voice was rougher than I expected. Unsteady.

She laughed. The sound was soft and musical. "I think you just tackled me into higher education."

And just like that—I was gone.

That moment—kneeling there on a college hallway floor, surrounded by scattered textbooks and her art—I knew. I knew.

I didn't just want to help her pick up her books.

I was keen to learn her story. I wanted to be in it.

She became my tranquility. She provided me with tranquility at the conclusion of my mission. Returning home brought me a sense of purpose, and the simple sounds of her typing on the laptop or humming in the kitchen transformed everything for the better. She understood that I served, but the nature of my division prevented me from disclosing specifics. However, the two-week mission I embarked on overwhelmed my sanity.

This is the reason I requested a discharge. Even when my thoughts veered off course, she consistently restored me.

She always had.

I needed someone to remind me I was human.

And lately… I had allowed everything to fade away. I'd watched her drift, and I hadn't fought for her. I'd been cold. Distant. Focused on work. Focused on staying in control—and in doing so, I'd lost the only thing that grounded me.

But she was slipping through my fingers.

Because of that fucking Zeff.

I clenched my jaw, the name igniting something deep in my gut. And Liliam… she was starting to look at him the way she used to look at me.

I couldn't lose her. Not when everything else felt like it was breaking apart.

If I could just get her back… If I could hold her, touch her, feel her warmth—I could come back from this. I could erase whatever the hell just happened.

She made me real.

And I needed that more than I'd ever needed anything.

13
THE KING

Zeff

The forest was alive with shadow.

I moved through the underbrush in silence, each step calculated, my senses razor-sharp. Gaius was there, guided by a scent that didn't belong. No. This one was worse.

It felt familiar and cocky.

A howl cut through the night—short, clipped. A warning from Aron. I was already shifting, muscles stretching and fur rippling along my spine, and in seconds, I was tearing through the woods.

I reached the clearing just as the trespasser emerged.

A tall, broad-shouldered wolf stepped out from the shadows; his light-brown fur was streaked with gold under the moonlight. And damn if he didn't pose—head high, tail flicked just so. The kind of entrance only one bastard could pull off.

He shifted mid-stride, casually, like he didn't give a damn whose territory he was in. When he stood in human form, that smug grin was already there, his sandy-blond hair tousled like it was styled for the cover of Alpha Quarterly. Naked, of course. And his eyes—his cold, silvery eyes—gleamed with trouble.

William Kane.

King of Alphas.

William Kane served as my training partner during my teenage years.

He was a man I both respected and resented equally.

William was always about the challenge. He was always pushing boundaries, measuring strength, and testing limits. That was in his blood. He came from a long line of Alphas—dominant, proud, revered. It was expected. It was tradition.

But fate isn't concerned about bloodlines.

His entire pack—his family—was slaughtered in a brutal territorial dispute. A massacre. His father, gone. Mates, elders, children—most dead or forced to flee into the cold night.

As dictated by our law, we opened our gates. We gave his survivors sanctuary. We made space for the broken pieces of what once was his legacy. But there's one truth that's never changed in our world:

There can only be one Alpha.

And William? He never forgot that. Never forgave it.

Even with his people taken in, even with food in their mouths and protection around them—he never stopped fighting me.

With every glance that said, "You're standing where I should be."

We trained side by side, bled together, and buried the past together. But underneath the bond was a storm that never settled.

Because deep down, William never joined our pack.

He was only waiting. For a time to rise again. For a crown he believed was his by right.

I also shifted, ensuring my movements were swift, clean, and dominant. When my feet hit the forest floor, I gave him a tight nod but didn't kneel this time. Screw that.

"Kane," I said coolly. "Lose your map?"

"Gunnolf," he greeted with a slow grin, stretching the word like it tasted good in his mouth. "Still brooding in the woods, I see."

"Still trespassing," I replied, voice flat.

His laugh was low and rich. "I missed you too."

Gaius snarled in my chest, but I kept my body still. Controlled.

"You're a long way from your throne," I said.

"Mm, yes," William said, pacing slowly around the edge of the clearing. "But word travels fast. And lately… your name keeps coming up. Not just in the council rooms." His eyes flicked to mine.

My jaw tightened.

He continued, "Imagine my surprise—hearing the ever-disinterested Gunnolf might've found his mate." He said the word with a hint of amusement, but I could see the curiosity beneath the façade. The hunger.

Aron, one of my young scouts, stepped forward in his gray wolf form, teeth bared. I flicked a hand, holding him back. William raised a brow at the gesture.

"Oh? No bow this time?" he teased. "What happened to manners?"

"They ran out the last time you 'dropped by' unannounced and nearly started a border war."

William chuckled. "Fair."

He stepped forward, arms spread like he expected a hug. I didn't move—but Gaius snarled low in my chest. "Careful."

He held up his hands. "I'm not here to fight you, Gunnolf. Not unless you ask nicely."

I stepped closer. "Why are you here?"

His voice lowered, threading the air between us with unease. "Something old is stirring. I've seen the vampires shifting. Gathering. They feel it too. They don't move like this unless destiny moved a piece on the board."

"I'm not the one who's always needed to prove something," I said.

William's smirk faltered for the briefest second.

Then he stepped forward, just once. Not threatening—just close enough to murmur, "When I find my Luna, I won't hide her in the trees."

I narrowed my eyes. "And when I claim mine, it won't be for show."

William's lips curve into a slow smirk. "So, you haven't claimed her yet."

I stiffened. "Stay out of my business."

"Your business is my kingdom, Gunnolf," he said, his voice sharper now. "You may have lost the crown, but don't think for a second I don't know what you're capable of."

Finally, William gave a small half-smile. "You and I—we don't like each other. But we need each other."

I stared at him, jaw tight. "Is that your way of saying you'll behave?"

His grin returned, sharp as ever. "No. But I'll warn you before I misbehave."

Finally, William gave a sharp, half-laugh. "Still sharp, Gunnolf. Still dangerous. Good." He stepped back, turning toward the trees. He didn't shift this time—he simply vanished into the dark.

Even though I remained motionless, my heart pounded in my chest.

He didn't know her name. But it was only a matter of time.

Why, I didn't know this, Josh! I mind-link my beta. *These are the types of things I should know firsthand!*

There was a small pause when Josh's reply came in. *I didn't. He didn't use any traditional procedures. He's not even staying in the Reservoir.* There was another pause, probably someone providing him information. *He's staying with the humans at AC Hotel Missoula Downtown.*

Fucking Williams. Leave it to him to break rules and to do things his fucking way. Arrogant Prick.

****

William

The moonlight sliced through the trees like silver blades, cold and relentless.

I walked with purpose, but I didn't shift. Sirius stirred beneath my skin, restless and sharp, but I didn't want the wolf tonight. He'd bring calm. Control. Logic. And I wanted none of that.

I needed to feel this way.

The anger. The confusion. The ache.

I stopped near the edge of the ridge, where a fallen log lay like a broken crown. Below, Gunnolf's territory sprawled out—peaceful, timeless. The kingdom was sculpted from a combination of rock and pine. Even from here, I could feel it humming with quiet power. His power.

The bastard always had good instincts.

I sneered, shaking my head. Zeff Gunnolf. He was the steady one. He was known for his calm demeanor. The one who never sought more than what was given. And now, the whispers said he was… mated?

My jaw clenched so tightly I felt my teeth grind.

"Bullshit," I muttered under my breath. "He wasn't even looking."

That's what burned the most. Zeff has never shown any yearning for his mate. During the countless nights we spent sparring, he never spoke as much as I did.

He hadn't called on the Moon with blood and breath like I had. He hadn't offered flame, bone, or sleepless prayers like I did. He hadn't searched.

And still… the wind shifted around him. The bond had awakened.

I'd heard it from a half-drunk priestess, eyes silvered and soul half-lost to starlight. She'd leaned into me at the edge of a fire and whispered, "Your rival's blood sings louder than yours now, my king."

The words hit me like a curse. I still hear them when I close my eyes.

I ran a hand through my hair, pacing near the edge. The forest was too quiet. The shadows are too loud. Sirius itched beneath my skin, and for once, I didn't let him out.

I needed to recollect the sensation of this moment.

The longing. The fury.

My feelings weren't due to Zeff having a mate.

I didn't have one. The Fucking King of Packs doesn't have one yet.

The moon still hadn't shown me my mate. It did not appear in a dream. It didn't manifest itself in a battle cry. Not in the Parr. My chest remained silent—cold where it should've burned.

And then, the air shifted again.

Carried on the wind, faint but unmistakable—

Vanilla.

I stopped breathing. I turned my head towards the breeze, my nostrils flared, and my heart began to race. That scent—warm, soft, and achingly sweet—pierced straight through me like a blade made of light. I knew that scent. I'd never smelled it in this world, but I knew.

It was hers. My Luna.

My mate.

My fingers twitched, claws threatening to rip through skin. Sirius surged forward, drawn to it like a moth to a flame. But still, I didn't shift. I couldn't. I just stood there, burning from the inside out.

"You're close," I whispered into the wind. "I know you're close."

But not mine yet.

And maybe not ever—because fate, in her cruel whim, had given Gunnolf what I'd begged for in silence.

I dropped down to sit on the log, pressing my fists against my knees. The forest stretched out before me, infinite and uncaring. I stared into the night, and I felt as if it were staring back at me.

"Is that how it works?" I asked. "The one who bleeds for her is ignored, and the one who stands still is chosen?"

There was no answer.

There was only the wind and the ache.

I looked down at my hands—hands that had built a kingdom, silenced enemies, and held the weight of a crown—but they were still empty. I continued to long for the one item that truly held significance.

If Gunnolf had found his Luna… everything was about to change.

The packers would feel the shift. So would the old blood. Even the vampires had started moving. Watching.

Waiting. And me?

I wasn't going to sit back and let fate rewrite the rules.

I stood, the fire in my blood burning brighter than ever. My mate was out there. And I would find her—to understand.

I was eager to see the woman who had the power to melt Gunnolf's heart.

I was eager to experience the taste of destiny.

And maybe, just maybe… to make the moon finally look my way.

****

Owen

The sink faucet roared as I scrubbed my hands under the freezing water, watching the blood swirl down the drain in thin, sickly spirals.

No matter how hard I scrubbed, it didn't feel clean. My skin burned from the friction. My knuckles were raw and reddened.

I stared at my fingers—flexed them—as if they didn't belong to me anymore.

What the hell happened?

I tried to piece it together, but my mind stuttered and blurred.

One second, I was standing in that sterile conference room, facing that bastard's too-smooth smile—

And the next—

Bodies. Blood.

My boots were slipping on the slick floor covered with blood.

A man gasping—Please, please, no—

Subsequently, the room fell silent.

My stomach twisted violently. I leaned over the sink, bracing my arms against the porcelain, trying to breathe.

This wasn't supposed to happen. I'd left this behind. I'd buried it deep the day I chose Liliam. I left everything behind that day.

What did he do to me?

I twisted the soap dispenser until it creaked under my grip, lathering again, scrubbing harder. Tiny flecks of blood splattered the mirror. I ignored them.

The water ran pink. The water supply was still insufficient. I kept scrubbing.

The buzzing in my ears grew louder, drowning out the sound of the faucet, the rush of water, the frantic pounding of my heart—

Suddenly, I heard a familiar voice.

Calm. Familiar.

"Hello, Owen."

I jerked upright, whipping around so fast I almost slipped.

The bathroom was empty. But the voice lingered, threading through the air like smoke. No—no, it wasn't possible. It couldn't be him. He was gone. He was dead.

I staggered back against the sink, the porcelain biting into my spine. My breathing came in short, ragged gasps.

"You didn't think it would be that easy, did you?"

The voice whispered again, closer this time, almost amused. I scanned the room, chest heaving, muscles locked and ready to strike—but there was no one there.

Only my own wild reflection, staring back at me from the mirror.

Eyes bloodshot.

Pale skin. Trembling hands.

One small red drop slid from my fingertip to the floor with a soft, accusing plip.

My knees threatened to give out.

This wasn't real. It couldn't be.

I grabbed the edge of the sink like a man clinging to the edge of a cliff, trying to anchor myself to something, anything.

"We're not finished yet, soldier."

The voice was right behind me now, so close I could feel the breath against my ear.

I slammed my fist into the mirror, shattering it into a web of broken reflections—shards catching my fractured face from every angle.

For a moment, there was silence.

Just the sound of water still running. Blood dripping. Pieces of my heart are breaking apart.

And in the wreckage of the mirror, between the broken slivers of myself, I thought I saw a flicker of red eyes. Watching. Waiting.

I staggered back, chest heaving, fists clenched so tightly my nails bit into my palms.

I had to get out. I had to find her.

Before, whatever was inside me—

Whatever they had woken up to—
Tore everything apart.

****

Liliam

The sound of keys jingling in the lock was the first warning.

Shadow, curled up by the window, lifted his head. His ears perked. His body stiffened.

Then came the click of the front door unlocking.

Shadow growled low, a deep rumble in his throat—not loud, but primal. His tail didn't wag. He stood, placing himself between the door and where I sat on the couch, laptop open but unread.

I stood too, suddenly tense.

The door opened slowly. And there he was.

Owen.

Looking… normal. He was wearing a tailored coat, his dress shoes were polished, and his hair was perfectly styled.

But his smile was wrong.

Like he'd practiced it in the mirror before walking in.

"Hey, Lil." His voice was soft, warm—too warm. "Missed you."

I blinked. "Hey… you're home early."

"Yeah." He dropped his keys into the bowl by the door and shrugged off his coat. "The install went quicker than expected. The client flaked halfway through."

A lie. I could feel it in my gut. Still, I nodded, watching him carefully as he walked toward me.

Shadow didn't move.

He stood stiff and silent, like a tiny sentinel.

"Hey, buddy," Owen said, crouching slightly, holding a hand out to Shadow. "It's me."

Shadow didn't approach. His lip curled just slightly—no bark, no snarl. Just… warning.

"Owen," I said gently, stepping forward. "He's still a little wary."

He stood up, his hand falling back to his side. "Still doesn't like me, huh?"

There was a flicker in his eyes then—too swift to name, but dark. He stepped toward me, pulling me into a sudden hug. His arms wrapped tightly around my waist, and I froze.

He was shaking. Just slightly.

And his scent… it was different.

There was still the cologne I recognized—Owen's familiar mix of cedar and mint—but underneath it now, something coppery. Metallic.

"I missed you," he murmured against my neck, and it didn't feel like a confession. It felt like a warning.

I leaned back instinctively, forcing a smile. "Are you okay?"

Owen cupped my face and kissed me.

Before, his kisses used to anchor me—warm, familiar, safe. But this?

This kiss felt off. Desperate. Possessive. His lips moved like they were trying to take something from me, not give.

I pulled away slowly, fingers curling at my sides.

"I love you so much," he whispered, his thumb brushing my cheek.

Shadow growled. Low. Fierce. The sound shook the soles of my feet. I reached down automatically to calm him, but my nerves were fraying.

Owen didn't flinch. He wrapped his arms around me tightly—too tightly—and lifted me off the ground.

I gasped, heart thudding, as an unnatural heat slithered across my skin. It wasn't arousal. It was pressure. Like being pulled under deep water.

He carried me toward our shared bedroom.

"Owen—"

My voice came out cracked and thin.

He pressed a finger to my lips. "Let me love you again, Liliam."

The door shut.

I heard Shadow's claws scrambling on the floor, his sharp whine behind the barrier.

"Owen, please—"

But something was wrong.

I couldn't focus. My thoughts dulled at the edges. My limbs felt disconnected from my will. I felt trapped in my own body, despite being present.

His hands were under my hoodie, lifting it. His eyes were intensely dark, no longer brown. Bronze is lit from inside. Burning. His hand reached out and pulled the necklace away.

I felt a pressure building behind my eyes. My chest tightened.

The air in the room thickened. It felt... warped. It felt as if I had stepped through a veil. The shadows lengthened. My skin prickled like I was being watched by something I couldn't see.

"I miss your presence so much," Owen said, his voice rasping like it was fraying from the inside. He pressed his face into my neck and inhaled, trembling. "You're mine, Liliam. You never stopped being mine."

His words didn't feel like devotion.

They felt like a curse.

I tried to move, but my body resisted. My lips were heavy, my tongue useless.

The situation isn't right. This isn't him.

He pressed me onto the bed, his weight more than it should be—denser, darker. Like something else had wrapped itself around his soul and was wearing his skin.

Shadow's muffled howls, desperate and wild, echoed from behind the door as the room engulfed me.

And the darkness took me.

14
MINE

Liliam

The moment I woke up, it felt like one of those brutal high school hangovers. My head throbbed; my vision was blurry as I struggled to focus on the room around me. The light was too bright. My mouth is too dry. The warmth of my skin overwhelmed me.

Then my gaze landed beside me.

Owen.

Tangled in the sheets, Owen slept on his stomach, his arm slung carelessly over my shoulder. His entire back was bare.

And so was mine.

Oh God.

Did we—?

Panic slammed into my chest. My memories from last night were fragments—nothing solid. Just flashes. Shadows. That pull. That pressure.

The last clear thought I had was lying down, a tightness curling in my chest like something was wrong. Then darkness.

I didn't remember saying yes. I didn't remember anything.

I swallowed hard, a bitter taste rising. My limbs moved before my mind caught up, scrambling out of the bed with shaking hands and bare feet. I didn't bother checking if he stirred. I just grabbed the first clothes I found and got out.

I opened the bedroom door and found Shadow curled against it, waiting. His ears perked immediately, and he whined—low, distressed, worried.

"I'm fine," I mumbled, though my voice was shaky and small. He didn't seem convinced.

I hurried past him, snatching my purse and keys from the living room, too nauseous to even think about breakfast.

I would rather not be there when Owen wakes up.

Couldn't.

I needed air. Distance. Clarity.

Down the street, there was a small café I liked. It was simple, offering warmth, coffee, and a space to relax. That was all I needed.

The bell above the door chimed as I stepped in. The scent of espresso hit me like a balm. The low hum of chatter and the clinking of cups felt normal. Safe.

I gave the girl at the counter a worn smile, ordered a black coffee and a breakfast croissant, and then tucked myself into a booth by the window. There was a small table set up for two people.

I wrapped my hands around the warm paper cup, letting the heat seep into my fingers. But inside?

Inside, I was unraveling.

What the fuck happened?

Then the door opened behind me—and something shifted.

It wasn't the temperature that changed. The sound remained unchanged.

Me.

It felt like a decline in barometric pressure. The universe seemed to take a deep breath.

My spine stiffened.

I glanced up, expecting—no—aching to see Zeff's familiar silhouette. But it wasn't him.

It was someone else.

Tall, messy-haired. He wore tailored black slacks, a storm-gray coat draped over his shoulders, and noiseless boots, as if he'd stepped out of a luxury noir film. The world seemed to pause for half a breath—then tilt slightly in his direction.

The light caught in his hair—sandy blonde, effortlessly tousled as though he'd dragged his fingers through it moments before stepping inside. His skin carried the warm light bronze of sun-kissed summers, glowing faintly against the crisp lines of his clothes.

But it was his face that held me captive.

His face, rugged and sharp-edged, was undeniably attractive in a way that was neither polished nor careful. It was the kind of beauty that threatened to be dangerous. His jaw was cut like stone, shadowed faintly with stubble, and when he grinned—because he did—two small dimples appeared, one on each side of his mouth.

It was… disarming. His boyish charm contrasted with the commanding, almost predatory stillness in his body.

He moved like a man used to getting what he wanted.

He moved with the confidence of someone who wouldn't hesitate to ask for what he wanted.

My breath caught in my throat before our eyes even met.

And when they did—

The sensation was akin to a sense of immobility.

Heat curled low in my stomach. Sharp. Uninvited. Wrong.

Zeff's presence ignited something warm and raw within me, akin to thunder wrapped in velvet.

This man's presence was colder. Sleek. I felt like a blade pressed gently to skin.

And he smelled.

The scent was that of passion fruit.

The scent was not synthetic but rather a genuine, sun-warmed fruit that was lush, wild, and decadent. The scent clung to him like a crown. Exotic. Commanding. My brain screamed danger, but my body… leaned in.

He cocked his head slightly, studying me like a riddle. His gaze dragged across my face, over my throat, lingering— not lewd, but deliberate. His lips curved into a slow, devastating smile.

"Is this seat taken?" he asked, motioning to the chair across from me in the booth.

I shook my head before I even realized I was moving.

He sat down like he'd been invited. He exuded a sense of belonging.

"I'm William," he said. His voice rolled across the table, smooth and smoky, like he could send it to match the timbre of your favorite songs. "You look like someone with a lot on her mind."

I tried to swallow, but my throat felt too tight.

"You could say that," I replied, my voice quieter than I meant.

His smile grew, but it didn't reach his eyes. Those eyes were ancient—strange, silver, with a weight to them. Beautiful. Terrifying.

He leaned forward slightly, his voice dipping low. "I'm excellent at listening."

I should've said no. I should've smiled politely, made up an excuse, and walked away.

But I didn't.

Because something inside me stirred. It wasn't exactly longing. It felt as if déjà vu, adrenaline, and hunger were intertwined into a single sensation.

And gods help me… I almost wanted him to stay.

He didn't speak again right away. He just watched me. Studied me.

And I hated that I didn't look away.

There was something about the way he looked at me—like he knew something I didn't. It appears he was anticipating a moment for a part of me to catch up.

The silence should have been awkward. But it wasn't.

The silence carried a weight.

I shifted in my seat, crossing my legs—then uncrossing them when the movement sent a subtle shiver through my thighs. My skin felt flushed and hypersensitive. It felt as if the air itself was piercing every exposed part of my body with its teeth.

I could feel the heat climbing my chest. My breath grew shallow.

What the hell is happening to me?

He tilted his head slightly, that same unreadable smile tugging at the corners of his mouth. "You're uncomfortable," he observed, his voice velvet smooth. "But curious."

My heart thudded.

"You don't even know me," I managed, though it came out more breath than voice.

His gaze dropped to my lips.

"No," he said. "But I will."

My pulse jumped. I gripped my mug like it might anchor me, but the ceramic felt too hot. Or maybe I was.

My thighs pressed together, a flicker of warmth pulsing between them. No. I clenched my jaw, tried to breathe through it, and then tried to bury it.

But his scent—damn it, that scent—coiled in the air, clinging to my senses like smoke in my lungs.

Zeff never made me feel like this. Zeff never made me feel like this.

With Zeff, it was like gravity. It felt like a force emanating from the depths of my soul. With William… it was like a whisper against the skin. The sensation of a finger tracing up the back of my neck was sensational. It was a gentle touch without any physical contact.

Wrong.

And yet—my body didn't care.

"I didn't catch your name," he said softly, interrupting my spiraling thoughts.

I hesitated. Every instinct told me to lie.

But something deeper—stupid and ancient—made me answer truthfully. "Liliam."

The name hovered between us, akin to a loaded gun.

He exhaled slowly, and for the first time, something shifted in his expression. His pupils dilated. His jaw twitched.

Like he'd just felt something. Like he recognized it.

I experienced a similar sensation when I first encountered Zeff.

But it was different. dangerous.Familiar—but colder.

I stiffened. "What?"

He blinked, and the mask slid back into place. "Nothing," he said, too casually.

But I didn't believe him.

For a brief instant, I was certain he gazed at me as if I were the solution he had been seeking.

And my skin erupted in goosebumps.

I needed to get out of there.

****

William

My breath caught the moment I laid eyes on her.

It wasn't just her face that captivated me; her beauty was undeniable. She exuded an untouchable beauty, akin to the moonlight shimmering on still water. The fragrance of vanilla struck me with a piercing intensity that captivated my mind.

It was what shifted inside me.

It was not the violent thunder I'd always imagined. It didn't feel like fate's grip on my chest.

It was quieter. Deeper.

It felt like the gradual movement of a key in a hidden lock. A pressure inside me is easing open.

Her energy brushed against mine like silk drawn across skin—too soft to be mistaken, too intimate to ignore. I paused mid-step, standing in the entrance of that café as if the air had been knocked from my lungs.

She looked up. Eyes locked.

Her breath hitched. And I felt it.

A subtle and low tug spiraled through my gut like smoke. She blinked quickly, as if trying to make sense of it, and in that instant, I knew she wasn't oblivious. She felt it too. Perhaps she didn't fully comprehend the situation. She sensed it, though it was not fully understood. The sensation was akin to the static that precedes a flash of lightning.

The scent of her lingered as she shifted in her seat. The scent was vanilla, not artificial, but real. Raw. The scent evoked memories of crushed orchids, warmth, and sunlit skin.

I swallowed hard, my hand twitching at my side. I hadn't reacted to someone like this in… hell, ever.

Was this what Gunnolf had felt?

The wild Alpha's blood burns now. I hadn't believed it.

But standing here, with that tug still threading itself around my ribs?

I believed it now.

Except… this wasn't a roar. This wasn't clarity.

It was temptation. The need for it was overwhelming.

And that was the most dangerous thing of all.

Because if this was it—if she was the one the moon promised me, the one I'd bled and waited for—then why did it feel more like a curse than a gift?

Why didn't I feel peace? Why did I feel hunger? And why, deep in my chest, did my wolf stay quiet?

Just… watching. Waiting.

I stepped closer, no longer sure if I was hunting the truth or daring it to hunt me.

She looked again, catching me staring.

And I didn't look away.

Not when I might've just found the one who would either balance me… or destroy me.

****

Liliam

The moment William sat across from me, the air in the café shifted. The sensation wasn't just energy. It was pressure.

It felt as if a weighty force touched my chest, sending a tingling sensation beneath my skin.

He watched me, like he was memorizing every blink, every breath. I tried to focus on the swirl of steam rising from my untouched coffee. I needed grounding. Normalcy. However, his presence was magnetic and overwhelming.

"So," William said smoothly, "do you always smell like vanilla, or is that just my luck?"

I blinked, caught between confusion and the inexplicable heat flushing up my neck. "That's… I—no, I mean, I don't know."

The bell above the door chimed.

I didn't even need to look. I sensed him.

Zeff.

His energy thundered through the room like a freight train without brakes. I'm sure I wasn't feeling like this. Is this his? I turned just as his eyes landed on us. William sat opposite me.

His gaze locked with William's.

And it was a war zone.

"Funny," Zeff said, stalking over like a storm in black denim and barely restrained fury. "Didn't realize we were taking meetings with royalty in public cafés now."

William leaned back in his chair, utterly unbothered. "What can I say? I enjoy mingling with the people. Especially the interesting ones."

Zeff's jaw clenched. His eyes flicked to me, softening for half a breath before hardening again when they returned to William. "Careful, Your Majesty. You're straying from your side of the map."

"I didn't know fate had borders," William said, sipping the espresso the barista had just placed. "Besides… I was just introducing myself to a fascinating young woman. You wouldn't want to be rude, would you?"

Zeff's body was taut with restraint. Barely.

"Fate doesn't give a damn about how smooth you are," he growled. "And she's not just anyone."

My breath caught.

William arched a brow, then turned to me slowly. "Is that so?"

I wanted to shrink into the floor—but I couldn't look away.

"Liliam," Zeff said, his voice lower now, gritted between teeth. "I've been calling you. Come, let's go."

The words hit me like a command. And I hated how much my body wanted to obey. But William spoke before I could move.

"She doesn't belong to anyone, Zeff," he said lightly, swirling his coffee like this wasn't a powder keg. "You should know better."

Zeff's laugh was cold. "She sure as hell doesn't belong to you."

"Then maybe," William said, rising slowly, "we should ask her who she'd rather spend time with."

Their eyes never broke contact. A current of energy passed between them—thick, primal, vibrating with something I didn't understand but felt down to my marrow.

And I was at the center of it. It hovered between fire and ice. Between two men who weren't just men.

And both men were looking at me as if I were the tether to something they couldn't afford to lose.

"We have to go, Liliam," Zeff said, his voice sharp but calm. Too calm. Zeff's calm was a precursor to an explosive event. His eyes never left William, locked in a glare that could've burned through steel.

But Zeff's urgency had little to do with time and everything to do with William.

I rose slowly, shoulders tight with confusion, pulse thumping in my throat. "You seem to know each other?" I asked, glancing between them. My voice was quiet, but it cut through the tension like a thread through silk.

William leaned back in his chair, utterly unfazed. "We do," he replied with that effortless arrogance, that glint of danger behind his silver eyes. "Way back. Isn't that right, Alpha?"

Zeff's jaw clenched at the title. His hand closed around my wrist—not harshly, but firmly enough to make me stumble slightly as he turned and started walking me toward the door.

"Back off, Kane," Zeff growled low, not bothering to look over his shoulder. "You've played enough games."

William's voice followed us like a shadow. "It's not a game if you feel it too."

I felt Zeff tense beside me. The moment we were out on the sidewalk, he let go of my wrist and raked a hand through his hair like he was trying to reset every nerve in his body.

"What the hell was that?" I asked, breathless.

Zeff looked at me, his jaw still tight, eyes unreadable.

"Someone who you shouldn't mess with," he muttered. The silence with Zeff was suffocating.

The silence didn't feel tense like a fight. It didn't feel awkward like a first date gone disastrous. No—this silence buzzed. The silence was as eerie as the air before a lightning strike. My pulse kept time with my footsteps, slow and steady. My thoughts were anything but.

Zeff hadn't said a word since he pulled me out of the café. He just walked—jaw tight, hands gripping like they were the only thing keeping him from tearing something apart.

But I didn't need words. I could feel it.

Whatever had happened back there—whatever unspoken challenge had passed between him and William— was a long-standing issue. And it wasn't over.

And the worst part?

The way William looked at me made my skin tingle. That could burn. I didn't understand. It felt like standing too close to a flame that provided no warmth.

It was nothing like Zeff.

Zeff's presence wrapped around me like heat. Like instinct. It felt right, even though it confused the hell out of me. But William... William's presence left me breathless. Off balance. This was unsettling, yet it wasn't something I could overlook.

I swallowed hard, staring at Zeff's profile. Strong jaw. Shadowed eyes. That faint twitch in his cheek muscle that only happened when he was trying not to explode.

"Are you going to tell me what that was about?" I asked softly, watching his knuckles whiten.

He didn't answer right away.

"No," he finally muttered, his voice low and gravel-edged.

That was his tell. When he was hiding something.

My gaze drifted to the sidewalk, but my reflection stared back at me with narrowed eyes. "Not today" didn't mean no. And that meant everything.

Because Zeff had secrets. And so did William.

And suddenly, all those things I used to laugh off in the romance books I read—shifters, bonds, moon mates—didn't seem so ridiculous anymore. The way Zeff looked at me was like he was always holding something back.

The way Shadow growled at Owen, like he saw something the rest of us didn't. How Owen pulled me into darkness. The way William smelled was like a dream I'd forgotten and made my skin buzz like I'd walked into another reality entirely.

Something wasn't adding up. But the numbers were getting close.

And if I was right... If even a sliver of what I was starting to feel turned out to be true...

Then I wasn't just caught between two men.

I was caught between *worlds*.

15
WARNINGS

The forest wasn't peaceful tonight.

It breathed around me—dark, pulsing, alive in a way that made the hairs on my arms rise. The trees loomed taller than I remembered, casting shadows too thick, too still. The silence wasn't comforting. It was a warning. The silence was a predator's hush.

I didn't know how I got here. One moment I was home… And the next, I was walking this winding path beneath the moon, boots crunching leaves that hadn't been there a second ago.

The cold pressed into me like damp, clutching hands, slipping beneath the layers of my clothes, worming along my spine. It wasn't just the temperature—it was the stillness, the way the night curled inward, quiet and waiting. There was a profound silence that resonated in my ears.

Then—snap.

A twig appeared, dry and deliberate.

I froze mid-step, my breath catching in my throat. The silence fractured.

Snap. Again. This time, the sensation was more intense.

My fingers clenched into fists at my sides as my gaze swept the dense wall of trees. Nothing moved. But I felt it—eyes. Watching. Stalking.

Crunch.

My heart kicked against my ribs.

Not one. The sensation was more intense than before.

The steps were slow. They were low to the ground. They were weighted not with carelessness, but with intention. It was as if whatever was out there wasn't afraid of being heard. It wanted me to know that it was coming.

I turned. Every movement felt foreign, like my limbs were borrowed, sluggish, and heavy, as if my blood had thickened into ice.

Then I saw it.

A flicker. A shimmer appeared between the trees just ahead—its eyes, wide and silver, capturing the meager light the moon was offering. The creature hovered close to the ground. Focused. Predatory.

A wolf. My breath hitched. But not just one.

To my right, the trees shifted again. Another form emerged from the dark—sleek, silent, and black as ink poured over muscle and bone. Its eyes weren't amber.

They were green. Its eyes radiated a green hue even in the absence of light.

They didn't snarl. They didn't rush. They watched.

The light brown wolf moved a step left, slow and confident. The blacks mirrored it to the right; their motions were so perfectly in sync that it felt choreographed. Predators are circling prey.

My feet refused to move. I found myself firmly planted on the ground, ensnared in the gradual rotation of an eons-old force—an entity I had no right to witness.

The forest had gone silent again. Even the wind didn't dare stir.

And there I stood, trembling in the eye of something I couldn't understand, my pulse pounding loud and frantic in my ears.

My throat closed. I couldn't move. Couldn't even scream.

The light brown wolf's lips curled back, exposing sharp teeth in a slow, deliberate snarl. It stalked forward—eyes locked on mine like I was already dead.

I backed up. Right in the line of the black wolf's path.

Except—he didn't lunge.

He stepped forward, positioning himself between me and the brown one, his body tense, muscles flexed. A sound rumbled from his chest—deep and commanding. It was a snarl that made the air vibrate.

The light brown wolf hesitated. Then attacked.

They collided with brutal force—bone and fur and fury. Claws scraped bark. Teeth sank. Growls thundered through the trees like earthquakes.

They were monsters, not just wolves—moving too fast, too precise. Each clash sprayed up soil. Snarls echoed like war drums. The light brown wolf's shoulder slammed into the black's ribs; the black countered with a crushing bite to the flank. It was savage, primal, and breathtaking.

And I couldn't move. I wanted to run, but my legs were cemented.

Then, just as the black wolf knocked the light brown one into the roots of an ancient oak, something worse happened.

The light brown wolf looked at me. Not at the black. At me.

The air thickened—pressed in like lungs filled with smoke. Every shadow twisted toward me.

The night held its breath, but my body didn't move. Couldn't move. The world screamed, "Run!" but I stood frozen, trapped in some terrible dream I hadn't meant to enter.

The light brown wolf rose from its crouch, muscles rippling beneath coarse fur. Step by step, it stalked toward me—deliberate. Measured. I was prey.

But the black wolf moved faster than thought—an obsidian blur slicing through moonlight. It slammed into the ground with a roar so deep and thunderous it shook the canopy above us, loosening birds from their branches.

They collided—again—but this time closer. Too close.

Claws raked. Fangs snapped. They tore into each other like enemies forged by fate. The sound of them—bone against bone, growls that split the air—was savage. Ancient. It was the kind of violence that didn't belong in the world I knew.

The black wolf twisted, yanking the brown one off balance with brutal strength. They tumbled across the forest floor, a tangle of rage and fur.

I stumbled backward, my legs finally remembering what fear was. The world began to tilt. My foot caught on a root—I fell hard, the wind knocked from my lungs as I hit the earth.

I braced myself for the next clash. For the end.

But suddenly—stillness.

The forest was silent again, like the trees themselves were listening.

The black wolf rose first, standing between me and the light brown one.

And then—he turned. His green eyes locked on mine.

My breath caught. In that instant, time fractured. His fur shimmered, rippling like waves beneath his skin. Then came the sound.

Crack.

The sound resembled a sharp break of bones. A twist. A groan. The flesh was contorting, the limbs reshaping, collapsing into something that was almost human—then fully human.

I couldn't look away. Couldn't blink.

The wolf became a man. Naked. Bleeding. Breathless.

Zeff stood where the black wolf had been, steam rising from his skin in the cool night air, his muscles tense with effort, with pain, and with fury. His chest heaved, his body trembling—but his stance never faltered. He continued to protect me.

Those green eyes, once wild, are now locked with mine—and softened.

"Run," he rasped. His voice was cracked stone, barely a whisper, almost a growl.

My lips parted in a scream that never came. I wanted to move. To breathe. I wanted to act.

But the world shattered—

And I woke up.

Gasping. I was drenched in sweat. Sheets tangled around me like vines. My heart slammed against my ribs like it was trying to escape.

I stared at the ceiling. I'm still trembling. Still there.

My body remembered the fear. My skin remembered the heat of his gaze. My ears still rang with the sound of growls.

I sat up slowly, running a shaking hand through my hair.

It was just a dream.

Except... It didn't feel like one.

Not with how real the dirt had felt under my hands.

It didn't feel as genuine as the dirt beneath my hands. And that voice— That voice wasn't from my imagination. It was Zeff's.

****

I blinked awake to the faint sound of humming. The house smelled… different. Warm. The scent wafted through the house, akin to butter and cinnamon, with a hint of effort.

I turned to find Owen standing at the bedroom door, smiling. "Good morning," he said, too softly.

I sat up slowly. "Hey," I said, remembering the night before. Owen acted as if nothing happened. Am I just exaggerating the situation?

"I made breakfast," he said, as if it were the most casual thing in the world. "Come on. Let's eat together."

That alone was enough to make my heart twist. He never did that—not since the early days. He had never done that before.

I followed him out of the bedroom, Shadow's tiny paws padding behind me, always at my side like a shadow of truth I couldn't ignore.

The kitchen was glowing with sunlight—and effort. Eggs. Bacon. Toast. Coffee. There was even a bowl of perfectly halved strawberries.

I blinked. "What's the occasion?"

Owen shrugged, flipping a towel over his shoulder with a little grin. "No occasion. You've been undergoing stress. I thought I'd do something nice."

I stared at him, unsure of what to say. I sat and touched the warm coffee mug in front of me, but my mind was spinning.

Shadow took his place beneath the table—until Owen sat down. Then came the growl. Low. Warning.

Owen frowned. "Seriously? Still?"

"He's just being cautious," I said quietly, nudging Shadow with my foot. He didn't move.

The meal tasted as delicious as it looked, but my stomach stayed tight. Owen kept talking—about work, about upgrades, about things that used to matter. He was trying; I could see that. And I wanted to appreciate it. I did.

But it all felt… practiced. He resembled a man attempting to cover up a sinister scene with the toast and the table arrangements.

Afterward, he stood and began clearing plates, speaking with a strange gentleness. "I know I haven't been myself. But I want to try, Liliam. I don't want to lose you."

His voice almost broke with that last word.

And for a moment, I felt that old ache again—memories of us before everything cracked.

"I appreciate it," I said softly. "I really do."

Then Shadow growled again—louder this time.

"Okay, seriously, what's wrong with this thing?" Owen snapped, his eyes flicking to the pup.

Shadow stood now, fur raised, teeth bared—not afraid but protecting.

I scooped him up, pressing his warm body to my chest. "He's just protective of me," I said. "He knows when something's… off."

Owen snorted. "Yeah, well, he needs to learn some boundaries."

So do you. I thought but didn't say.

As I turned toward the hallway, Shadow nuzzled closer to my neck, his little heart thudding fast against my collarbone.

I caught my reflection in the hallway mirror, Shadow tucked against me like a warning.

And in that moment, my mind flashed to Zeff—his eyes, his warmth, the feeling in my chest when he was near.

With Owen… it felt like a memory trying to resuscitate itself.

But with Zeff… it felt like the beginning of something I wasn't ready for—but couldn't turn away from.

16
LUNA

Liliam

The soft clack of my keyboard filled the otherwise quiet office. I should've been finishing the report my manager had assigned me this morning—but my mind was elsewhere. Again.

I couldn't stop thinking about the dream.

The dream, or whatever it was, captivated me.

Two wolves. The first wolf was black, while the other was light brown. The wolves' bodies circled like storm fronts about to collide. I had stood frozen in the forest, the trees humming like they knew something. And when the fight erupted, it wasn't chaos—it was deliberate. Like a war older than memory.

The black wolf… He'd stepped in front of me. Protected me. Bared his teeth, took the hits, and refused to let the light brown one reach me. And he turned into Zeff.

William has known Zeff way back, and William's hair is sandy blonde. It bears a striking resemblance to light brown.

The similarities were too much of a coincidence.

I opened a new tab and typed:

"Black and brown wolves fighting in dreams meaning"

Most of it was vague, spiritual fluff. Loyalty. Inner conflict. Protection. But nothing explained the sharpness. The clarity. It felt heavy in my chest, as if I were witnessing something genuine.

I didn't even hear Zeff approach until I felt his presence—warm and unnervingly attuned—leaning just enough over my shoulder to see the glowing search bar.

"What are you looking at?" he asked, sipping from his water bottle like it was just another day.

I slammed the laptop shut instinctively. "Nothing."

He quirked an eyebrow.

"Okay, fine. "Dreams," I muttered, then added, "about wolves."

Zeff choked.

I mean, literally, choked. Water shot from his nose, and he doubled over, coughing so violently I thought he was going to collapse. I jumped up from my seat and reached for a napkin.

"Jesus, are you okay?" I asked, wide-eyed.

He waved me off, still coughing, eyes watering.

"I'm fine," he rasped after a beat, though his voice was strained and his posture a little too stiff. "Just went down the wrong pipe."

Yeah. Right.

I sat back down, eyeing him. "It was just a dream," I said carefully, like I was prodding at something delicate. "Two wolves. One black. One light brown. They fought. The black one was… protecting me. The other one felt wrong. Hostile. I don't know. It just felt real."

Zeff had gone very still. Too still.

His face had lost some of its color, and his jaw remained fixed. His hands clenched the edge of the desk like it was the only thing keeping him grounded.

"And… that's all?" he asked, his voice low.

I narrowed my eyes. "Why? Does that sound familiar to you?"

His throat bobbed in a swallow, and he avoided my gaze. "Dreams are… symbolic. Stress. Subconscious junk. You've been going through a lot."

"You're deflecting."

His intense gaze snapped to meet mine in response. Intense. Caught.

"Liliam," he said slowly, carefully. "If it ever became something you needed to know… I'd tell you."

It wasn't a no.But it wasn't a yes either.

And I could see the storm behind his eyes—the way his shoulders tensed, like he was holding something back. It was as if someone understood the significance of my dream.

I sat back slowly, heart thudding. "You're scared."

His jaw tightened. "No."

"You are," I whispered, more to myself than to him. "You know something. Zeff… Are you saying it's not just a dream?"

His silence was enough to answer. And suddenly, Shadow's reactions made sense. Zeff's aroma soothed him.

Two wolves. One fight. One protector.

My hand curled into a fist in my lap. I didn't know what I was uncovering—but I was close. Zeff was making every effort to postpone the revelation of the truth.

However, the dream had already started to reveal itself.

And I wasn't going to stop until I dug all the way through.

****

I didn't want to bother Owen today, especially considering his new resolution to "fix our relationship." I should be grateful, but after everything with Zeff, Owen was the least of my worries.

So, I slipped on a pair of comfortable boots and decided to walk to work. Clear my head. Feel human again.

Shadow, of course, wasn't having it.

He pawed and whimpered at the door as I gently shut it behind me, the doggy door already locked. His muffled, indignant howl echoed behind me—more husky drama than wolf growl—and guilt tugged at me. But I needed space. Silence. I desired a world where no one attempted to alter me, manage me, or take ownership of me.

The truth was my life had always felt hollow. Quiet. Predictable. I had Owen. I had work. That was it. I had no close friends to confide in. There were no hidden aspirations. Just... survival in soft beige.

But Zeff flipped the entire pallet. Being wanted—truly wanted—had woken something up in me. It felt as if my body and soul had been asleep, and he had spoken the language that awakened them.

And now... the dreams. The pull. The heat lingered like fingerprints pressed into my skin.

I was unraveling. And I didn't know if I was ready for the truth I could feel coming.

"I knew I'd find you here."

The voice wrapped around me like velvet over steel. The man I somehow already knew effortlessly caught my phone in midair as I jumped.

William.

My entire body tensed, every instinct screaming danger—but something else sang in my blood. Something carnal. Terrifying.

"William?" I managed, my voice thinner than I liked.

He offered a slow, elegant bow, then took my hand before I could react. His lips brushed the back of it with maddening gentleness.

"Madam," he murmured.

Fireworks. Electricity. His touch wasn't like Zeff's—warm and anchoring. William's touch was sharp and charged, like the promise of lightning just before it strikes.

"What are you doing here?" I asked, trying to sound composed.

He didn't release my hand as he returned my phone. "Interacting with a beautiful woman," he said smoothly, as if it were the most obvious answer in the world.

My lips parted to reply, but his grin silenced me. A smirk, both lazy and knowing, etched a half-dimple into his cheek.

"I couldn't possibly let anything happen to you on your walk," he said, his tone low and silk-wrapped.

"It's eight a.m.," I pointed out, dryly.

"You can never be too careful," he countered, gesturing for me to continue walking.

So, I did. And he walked beside me. Every inch of my body was aware of him—too aware. The breeze carried his scent—the dark and sweet passion fruit laced with heat—and my mouth went inexplicably dry.

I didn't want to be drawn to him. I shouldn't be. But somehow, I was. Not in the same way I felt about Zeff—Zeff made me feel safe. His presence felt like a temptation.

"Have you lived in Montana long?" he asked, breaking the silence with casual charm.

I blinked at the question. "Um—three years. I moved for work."

He nodded, eyes glinting silver in the morning light. "That explains it."

"Explains what?" I asked, my voice tentative.

His gaze lingered a moment too long. "Why our paths never crossed."

There was weight to that answer. Not flirtation—something else.

I hesitated, then pushed, "You seem to know Zeff."

He let out a soft laugh, smooth and rich. "Gunnolf and I go back to our teens."

The name struck me. Powerful. Wild. I hadn't even known it before now.

"I moved here after…" William paused, his tone dipping. "A loss in the family. Tragic accident. I found my place in the community here."

His eyes were on the path ahead, but there was a shadow in them.

"We've always been competitive," he continued. "After all, we were—" He stopped again, this time his gaze narrowing as it slid toward me. "How much do you know about Gunnolf?"

My breath hitched at the question. How much did I really know?

He's strong. Kind. Intense. Addictive. He is the man of my dreams. He is the man I yearn to embrace and never let go of. He is the one who causes my entire body to ache.

I barely knew how to describe him—only that I felt him. And now, standing here with William, everything was getting harder to explain.

"Not much," I said quietly, my voice barely carrying over the hum of traffic. "We met at work. And since then, we've… spent time together."

A slow smile curved William's lips, deliberate and unreadable. But it didn't touch his eyes. Those silver eyes stayed fixed on me like a blade to my throat—unblinking, dangerous, ancient.

"I see," he murmured.

And then his hand—elegant, strong—glided over my shoulder. I tensed, but before I could react, he pulled me toward him with effortless strength. His face was suddenly inches from mine, his breath brushing my lips. I inhaled sharply.

His grin deepened.

"I can be the man you want me to be," he said, voice low, deep, and too intimate for a street corner.

And then—he kissed me.

It wasn't soft. It wasn't sweet. It was a mix of heat, hunger, and claiming.

His mouth crashed into mine with a force that stole the breath from my lungs. My fingers twitched, wanting to push him away, but the shock of it—the raw electricity of it—froze me in place.

His lips were fire, his body pressed close, too close, and all I could feel was him. I could taste the sweet and tangy flavor of passion fruit from his lips. The kiss poured through me like molten sugar—thick and slow and burning. My skin lit up with sensation, every nerve ending alive, every inch of me aware of how dangerous this was. The danger he posed was palpable.

And yet—I kissed him back.

The kiss lasted only for a heartbeat. Maybe two.

But it happened. The moment of surrender was filled with shame and confusion.

His hand cupped the side of my neck, fingers splayed like he was marking me, his touch both possessive and coaxing. He tasted like temptation and thunder, like something ancient wrapped in silk

My body ignited. I could feel it—this heat building in my core, spreading through my limbs, making my knees go weak and my stomach flutter and my lungs forget how to breathe.

Then the moment broke. Sanity slammed back into me like cold water.

I gasped, shoving against his chest. "What the hell—"

His expression was smug. Dangerous. Almost pleased. His silver eyes gleamed with triumph.

But beneath that… something darker flickered. His scent still clung to me like a brand—sweet, thick, unshakable. But his hand didn't let go of my arm. It felt like a blazing fire of desire clinging to my skin.

And then—

A black SUV pulled up beside us with a low purr.

William's reaction was immediate. His eyes flashed, and a sound rose from his throat—a low, guttural growl that didn't belong in this world. The sound echoed through my spine, resembling the pounding of thunder in my bones.

The car door opened. A tall man stepped out, his suit immaculate, his expression unreadable.

"Your Majesty," the man said, bowing slightly. Then he opened the passenger door, holding it with practiced precision.

Your Majesty?

The words echoed in my skull.

William didn't move at first. He stared at me, that same strange heat simmering beneath his skin. It felt as if he didn't want to let go.

He released me slowly, fingers trailing from my arm like he was trying to imprint something into my skin.

"I shall see you around," he said softly

Then, with a flicker of a smile—too sharp to be kind—he added, "My Luna."

He slipped into the SUV, and the door closed with a final, echoing click. The vehicle glided away, leaving me frozen on the sidewalk.

My heart pounded against my chest.

Luna? Your Majesty?

What the hell was going on?

I stood there, breathless and shaken, arms wrapped around myself as if to hold something in.

It was all beginning to unravel. My thoughts. My understanding of this. Of them.

This was something much, much bigger.

****

William

The SUV purred steadily beneath me, its interior dim and cool, but my mind was a wildfire—raging, uncontrollable.

I could still feel her.

It was not just the scent that clung to me like a brand but also the raw energy that hummed beneath her skin. The second my fingers brushed her shoulder, when I pulled her close, it was like grabbing a live wire. Quiet power. Controlled chaos. It was not the roaring fire I had always expected from finding my mate—rather, it was a slow, searing burn that devoured everything in its path.

And the kiss?

Gods.

It wasn't just heat. It was the truth.

Her lips met mine in a collision of hesitation and instinct, resistance and craving. It had been a mistake—my mistake. I shouldn't have kissed her. I shouldn't have taken that moment.

But I had. And it was the most satisfying, dangerously addictive thing I'd ever tasted. For one breathless second, she kissed me back. It was there. The surrender. The pull. That spark that sang down my spine like prophecy made flesh.

A jolt of something ancient had surged through me the moment our mouths met—a recognition older than memory, deeper than instinct. It wasn't lust alone. No, the heat between us was undeniable, but what burned hotter was the certainty.

Power recognized power.

I had touched countless women in my life—tasted sweetness, deception, and fleeting devotion. But her? Her soul moved under my hand. Stirring. Awakening.

And she didn't even know. Not yet.

But when she pulled away—trembling, flushed, shocked—I saw the fear in her eyes… and the hunger she was trying so hard to bury. It stirred something possessive inside me.

I leaned forward, bracing my elbows against my knees, staring out at the dark blur of trees flying past the tinted window. My fingers still tingled from the contact, the echoes of that silent crackle of magic that lived in her blood.

She was more.

She is more

And Gunnolf? That bastard hadn't told her a damn thing.The realization festered inside me like poison. He hadn't marked her. Hadn't claimed her. He hadn't whispered the truth into her ear under the moonlight as she deserved.

No—he kept her in ignorance. He shielded her from the truth.

Perhaps this was done to safeguard her. Or maybe because he doubted he deserved her.

A slow, cruel smile curved my mouth.

Good. Let him doubt. Doubt served as a gateway, and I was determined to step through it.

I saw the flicker of uncertainty in her eyes—the way she looked at me and questioned everything she thought she knew about Gunnolf and about herself. That was the beginning. That marked the initial breach in the barrier Gunnolf had constructed.

I would widen it. I would be the one to give her answers. I would provide her with the truth.

Let her wonder why Gunnolf hid who he truly was.

Let her ache with confusion and the slow-burning hunger only I could stoke. Let her remember my touch when her dreams turned wild and restless. I exhaled a long, slow breath, savoring the satisfaction curling in my chest.

"You've kept her in the dark, Gunnolf," I murmured to the faint reflection in the glass, my silver eyes glinting back at me, feral. "And in darkness… things begin to bloom."

And when she bloomed—

I would be there.

The sun. The storm.

Whatever she needed was there. Whatever would tear her from Zeff's hands and into mine.

The driver cleared his throat, his voice cautious. "The Council is asking for your return, Your Majesty."

I didn't move for a long moment.

Then, with a slow growl vibrating in my chest, I leaned back against the seat, rage simmering just beneath my skin.

"Fuck the Council," I said, my voice sharp and venomous.

My fists curled at my sides, nails biting into my palms.

Since the day I was crowned king, they had tried to chain me—dressing their control up in traditions and laws so old they stank of rot. Even after two years of my eight-year reign, they closely monitored every move I made. Questioned.

Change one law? They screamed.

Challenge an ancient rite? They clawed.

Demand modernization? They threatened.

And now? Now they dared to pressure me into mating for appearances, to appease the other Alphas' fragile pride.

"Balance," they said. Every king needs a Luna.

I could practically hear their whining voices in my skull.

No. I wouldn't take some carefully chosen pawn, paraded out like a prize.

If I took a mate, it would be Liliam.Only her. Because when I touched her...

When I smelled her, when I gazed into her wide, storm-tossed eyes...I knew.

She was mine. She was not bound by the traditions.

She belonged to me, not to Gunnolf.

To me.

And no one—no gods, no council, not even Gunnolf—was going to stand in my way.

17
REALIZATION

Liliam

I sat at my desk, fingers hovering uselessly over the keyboard, the document on the screen blurring into nothing. The cursor blinked at me—a cold, relentless reminder of how stuck I was. How lost.

I should be working. I ought to maintain focus. Instead, my mind betrayed me—again. It drifted, unbidden, back to him.

The memory returned to Zeff. The memory wasn't kind. It didn't come softly. It crashed into me—raw, vivid, and overwhelming.

The heat of his body pressed into mine. His hands coiled around my waist, expressing both reverence and possessiveness simultaneously. The low growl of his breath against my ear ignited every nerve in my body.

My skin ached to be closer, to lose myself in him, to drown in that impossible, magnetic pull.

It wasn't just touch. It was something inside me, clawing to move closer.

God, the way he made me feel— Seen. Wanted.

The universe seemed to bend around me the moment he gazed at me. I bit down on my lip, the ache in my chest too much. My body knew before my mind did.

I knew Zeff was different. He meant something.

And yet—

My treacherous longing summoned the devil himself— William's face flickered behind my eyelids.

William's silver eyes were captivating. William's smile was slow and devastating. Where Zeff was warmth—an inferno that wrapped and consumed—

William embodied a unique essence.

A storm. A tempest. Powerful. Icy. His all-consuming nature caused my soul to shudder. I remembered the way he had pulled me close, his hand sliding over my skin like silk over fire. The pulse of energy that had jumped between us at the smallest touch—like tasting forbidden magic.

The way my breath had hitched without permission, my body leaning forward before my mind could scream no.

Temptation.

It had whispered through me like a drug

William was dangerous and dressed in elegance. And some dark, broken part of me wanted to touch it. I wanted to touch it, to see if it would burn me to ashes.

A sharp pang of guilt twisted my stomach.

Owen.

I slammed my eyes shut, forcing a long, ragged breath into my lungs.

Owen—who had once made me feel safe. Steady. Loved.

But now?

Now, when I thought of him, all I felt was… emptiness and darkness. It was akin to grasping for a familiar object—only to discover its hollowness.

I hated myself for it.

For feeling too much for one man who had never touched me wrong. And I felt too much for two others who had barely begun to touch me at all.

What the hell was wrong with me?

I pressed my palms into my eyes, trying to stop the images, feelings, and ache that reason couldn't bury.

This wasn't just an attraction. It wasn't just loneliness.

It was something bigger. Unknown threads within me began to tug. I dropped my hands into my lap, staring blankly at the notepad on my desk. The scribbled half-sentences mocked me.

"You're losing yourself," a small voice whispered inside.

Maybe I was.

Maybe it had already begun the second Zeff touched me. Or maybe it started the night William's eyes pinned me to the earth and left me gasping for air I didn't understand.

I swallowed hard, the weight of it almost too much.

I plopped down onto the room floor, crossing my legs as Shadow padded over, tail wagging softly. I stared at Shadow, who cocked his head at me, big brown eyes wide and patient.

"You're the only one I can talk to," I whispered, running a hand over his soft fur.

He licked my palm once, as if to say, "I'm listening."

I sighed. "Okay, so… hear me out."

Shadow gave a tiny whine, settling onto his haunches, as if bracing for one of my infamous rants.

"I know it sounds crazy. Like, certifiably crazy." I rubbed my face with both hands. "But what if… what if they're not just… people?" My voice dropped to a whisper, as if someone could hear. "What if Zeff and William are something else?"

Shadow tilted his head again, that little quirk that always made him look like he understood too much.

"I mean…" I laughed awkwardly. "You've seen Zeff. How strong he is. How… other he feels sometimes. And William? His movements and scent suggest that he is trying to control the air around him."

I leaned forward, grabbing two of Shadow's chew toys from the floor—a stuffed fox and a worn, grinning wolf plushie.

I sat them down in front of Shadow dramatically.

"Alright, Professor Shadow. Today's lesson: Supernatural Suspicions 101," I said, my voice trembling between humor and something closer to fear.

I tied a little ribbon around the fox's neck. "This one's Zeff," I said, tapping it.

Then I wrapped a scrap of blue thread around the wolf toy. "And this one's William."

Shadow wagged his tail, looking between the two toys.

"Okay, buddy," I said, heart thudding in my chest. "Who should I trust?"

I expected him to lunge straight for Zeff's toy. He obeyed and loved Zeff. I loved Zeff. It would make sense.

But Shadow hesitated.

He shifted his paws awkwardly, his ears flattening back against his skull. His gaze flickered between the two toys, then up to me—so sad, so torn it made my throat tighten.

Then, with a whimper so soft it was almost a breath, he nudged the toy labeled William.

I froze, staring at him, my hands curling into fists on my knees. Shadow whined again, licking the toy once before sitting back, his tail tucked low, his whole body radiating unease.

"No…" I breathed, shaking my head. "You can't be serious."

Shadow tucked his snout against my knee, pressing into me like he could apologize, like he could explain without words.

"But why?" I whispered, stroking his head. "Why him?"

Was Shadow warning me?

Or… was he saying William would win? I barely knew the person.

The thought pierced my stomach like a knife.

I pulled the toys away, heart hammering. "Maybe you're just confused, huh?" I said, forcing a laugh that came out strangled. "Maybe you just liked the smell."

Shadow didn't answer, of course. He just rested his head on my leg and stared up at me with those big, mournful eyes, and somehow… that was worse than words.

Because deep down, in the place I would rather not look at too closely, I already knew.

Something was happening.

I was unable to stop it.

And regardless of which toy Shadow picked… it wouldn't save me from the choice I would eventually have to make.

Between the one who felt like home…Or the one exuded a sense of strength.

I glanced over at the clock. It was just 9 pm. Owen wasn't back after eleven. It was late, but not too late to go for a walk, to clear my head, to try to sort through this mess. Maybe some fresh air would help.

I stood up, grabbing my coat and heading for the door. As I walked through the house, Shadow trotted over, looking up at me with wide, curious eyes. "Come on, Shadow," I said, smiling despite myself. "Let's go for a walk. I need to think."

****

The streets were eerily quiet as I neared the park. The stillness wasn't peace—it was suffocating, thick like fog pressed against my skin. Every instinct screamed at me to turn back. But I didn't. I was worn out. I needed air. I needed clarity.

That was my first mistake.

I heard them before I saw them.

Drunken laughter. The laughter was sharp and broken. Male.

My stomach coiled, breath catching. I reached down instinctively, brushing my fingers against Shadow's fur. He trotted beside me, his ears already perked, his small body tense with unease.

"Hey, pretty lady," a voice slurred, too loud in the hush of night. "Where are you going all alone?"

I didn't answer. I refrained from looking. My hands tightened around my sides as I kept walking, faster now. Don't engage. Don't feed them attention.

"Don't ignore us!" Another called, voice louder, closer. "We just want to talk!"

No, you don't. You want something else. You want my fear. My throat tightened as I risked a glance over my shoulder.

Mistake. Two of them were following. Staggering, grinning. Predators in borrowed skin. Shadow's growl started low, deep, and unnatural for his size. The primal sound raised the hairs on my neck.

"Hey!" One-lunged.

His hand clamped around my wrist like iron. I gasped, stumbling.

"Let me go!" I shouted, my voice breaking.

He reeked of sweat and stale beer. His other hand reached for me, his touch possessive, obscene. "Not until we get to know each other better, sweetheart."

I twisted in his grip, panic flaring in my chest. "Stop it! Let me—!"

Shadow barked—no, snarled—and lunged. His teeth sank into the man's ankle. The movement was swift and unstoppable.

The man howled in pain. "You little—!"

A kick. Shadow's body struck the ground with a sickening thud.

"Shadow!" I screamed, my heart tearing in two. He yelped, curling in on himself, whimpering.

The second man laughed, grabbing my waist from behind. "Feisty," he muttered against my ear. "Bet you taste just as sweet."

"Get your hands off me!" I shrieked, flailing, trying to kick, trying to scream louder—but my voice was lost to their laughter. This is why I never liked walking at night. This is why Owen complains when I go alone.

"You smell wonderful," the first one groaned, dragging me closer. "Shit. What are you hiding?"

His lips brushed my neck. My skin crawled.

The third man stepped in front of me, holding a cracked bottle by the neck. "Let's take her somewhere quieter."

I tried to fight—scratching, twisting—but another hand clamped over my mouth. Their bodies pressed in, heavy and suffocating. Shadow forced himself up once more, growling despite his shaking legs. His little body trembled, his fur bristling with fury and pain.

He charged again. Another kick—this one landed with a crack. Shadow cried out, collapsing.

I couldn't breathe.

"Shadow! No!" My scream ripped from my throat, wild and broken. "Please, stop! Please!"

Tears streamed down my face. My limbs shook. The strength in me waned under the weight of horror and helplessness. Someone was going to hurt me—badly, perhaps. Maybe worse.

Then, a voice emerged.

"Gentlemen."

The voice sliced through the chaos like a blade.

Smooth. Controlled. The men froze.

Footsteps echoed in the silence, deliberate and calm. From the shadows beneath the park lamp, a figure stepped into the light.

The figure was tall and composed, and his power rippled beneath each step like coiled lightning

William.

His silver eyes shimmered like moonlight over ice. He looked at them the way a lion might look at trespassing jackals—amused, but entirely unimpressed.

"That," he said, his tone silk over steel, "is no way to treat my Luna."

The man gripping me scoffed, but I felt him stiffen. "Who the hell are you supposed to be?"

William ignored him. His gaze slid to me—his eyes darkened, nostrils flaring slightly, like he was breathing in something intoxicating.

He was calm, but a terrifying calm. Not detached. Calculating.

"Let her go," he said softly. "Before I stop asking nicely."

One of the men took a step forward. "We don't need—"

He didn't finish. William moved like liquid rage. One second, he was five feet away. Next, he had the man by the throat, lifting him with one hand as if he weighed nothing. His grip was effortless, but I could hear the choke and see the man's feet dangling.

"I said," William growled, his voice dropping to something otherworldly, "let her go."

The man behind me released me immediately. I stumbled back, gasping. Shadow whimpered near my feet, and I dropped to my knees, scooping his trembling body up, cradling him to my chest.

Everything was happening so fast. William tossed the man aside like a ragdoll. He hit the ground with a groan.

William turned his head slightly, regarding me with a small, unreadable smile. "Don't worry, my Luna," he said. "It's all taken care of."

That word again. Luna.

"You don't—" I started to say something, but he turned away from me and began stalking the others.

They tried to run. They didn't get far. He was a blur. Bone crunched. Screams echoed. In the shadows, he moved like death itself. Calculated. Cold. Beautifully monstrous.

Blood hit the pavement in bursts.

And yet… my heart wasn't afraid in the way it should have been. It was pounding, yes—but it wasn't fear. It was recognition. Like part of me knew what he was.

I understood what both represented.

Then came the growl.

Low. Deep. It vibrated through the air, through the ground, and through me.

I turned slowly.

A massive black wolf stepped into the clearing, fur like shadow, eyes glowing with a savage, green fire.

My heart stilled.

I knew it before I could name it. That was the wolf from my dreams. It was the wolf who circled to protect me. He was the one who kept a close watch. He transformed into Zeff.

My breath caught as he growled again—not at me, but at William.

William chuckled, licking blood from his lip. "Aren't you a little late, Alpha Gunnolf?"

His growl deepened, and then—before I could think—William began to change.

His bones cracked, reshaping. His skin split, fur spilling forth. I stared, frozen in place, as he became the light brown wolf from my dream. Massive. Regal. Terrifying.

The two wolves stood in tense silence, their powerful forms silhouetted under the pale wash of the streetlamp. The black wolf exuded raw power—his body lean and muscular, fur bristling like a storm ready to break. His emerald eyes glowed with primal fury, locked onto the light brown wolf before him. William, now a hulking beast with light brown fur and silver-ringed eyes, crouched low, a menacing snarl curling from his throat.

Then they lunged.

The impact was a thunderclap—bone and sinew colliding with force that reverberated through the ground. Zeff slammed into William's side, driving him backward, claws raking across his opponent's flank. Tufts of fur flew as their bodies twisted in a flurry of savage motion. The sound of snarling and snapping jaws echoed like thunder in the park's silence.

William retaliated, his massive frame whipping around with terrifying speed. He sank his teeth into Zeff's shoulder, eliciting a sharp, pained growl. But Zeff didn't falter. He twisted beneath William's grip, his jaws clamping down hard on William's foreleg. The light brown wolf yelped, and the two broke apart briefly—circling each other like predators, eyes locked, muscles rippling beneath their coats.

They clashed again.

This time, they rose on hind legs, raking at each other with claws that slashed deep. The dim light revealed blood-darkened patches of fur, slick and gleaming. Zeff's fangs snapped inches from William's throat, while William retaliated with a brutal headbutt that sent Zeff staggering.

More than just instinct drove every strike—it was personal. Rage pulsed in every movement. Territory. Power. Her.

They fought not just as wolves, but as rivals.

William lunged, trying to overpower Zeff with brute strength, but Zeff ducked low, driving his shoulder into William's ribs and flipping him onto his back. The light brown wolf snarled and scrambled upright, his hackles bristling as saliva dripped from his bared teeth. Their growls became a language of their own—ancient, primal, and full of challenge and warning.

Sparks of magic laced the air, static buzzing through the night. I could feel it—tangible, like storm winds pressing against my skin.

I sat frozen, yet my heart screamed for it to stop. "Please," I whispered. "Please stop."

But they didn't hear me. Or maybe they couldn't.

The wolves collided again—black and brown, fury and force—slamming into each other with a final, earth-shaking impact that seemed to crack the world open around me. Claws tore across fur, teeth snapped inches from throats, and growls thundered in my chest like drums of war. The sound was too real. The sight is too raw.

My mind screamed it louder now, refusing to be silenced.

Werewolves are real. This is real.

Zeff was the black one. William was the light brown one.

I knew it. In the marrow of my bones, in the blood rushing wild through my veins. The one who had touched me, held me, kissed me, and fucked me—he wasn't just a man.

My heart galloped. My lungs couldn't catch up.

No, no, no, this isn't possible. But it was. It was happening. It was unfolding directly before me.

My body began to tremble violently, like something inside me had been turned upside down. The fabric of my reality appeared torn apart and reassembled incorrectly. My skin prickled, hot and cold all at once. My fingertips tingled with panic. I couldn't move, couldn't scream—only feel. Feel the fear, the betrayal, the awe, and the pull.

He was real. They were real.

Something like lightning surged through me—raw, electric, and almost unbearable. My head spun. My vision blurred. The air thickened, heavy and charged, like I was submerged in something not quite water, not quite magic—but drowning all the same.

I looked down. And the world changed.

Threads of light enveloped my once familiar hands. Thin. Translucent. Alive. They danced around my fingers like silk caught in the wind, spinning tighter, weaving patterns I didn't understand. But I could see them.

Feel them.

They pulsed against my skin with a low, thrumming hum—like a heartbeat, like a warning. The energy vibrated around me, through me, building faster and louder. My skin buzzed. My nerves sparked. Every part of me felt as though it was breaking apart.

The threads flared brighter—amber-gold, blinding—until my entire vision was filled with light.

And then, everything went black.

To Be COntinued

ACKNOWLEDGEMENTS

I want to express my deepest gratitude to everyone who has supported and walked beside me on this incredible journey.

To my amazing community at **Inkitt**, thank you for standing by me—from the earliest drafts to this final step. Your encouragement has meant the world.

A special thanks to my fellow local authors, **Valeria and Gloria Gonzalez** and **Raymond Vollmond**, whose unwavering support and motivation reminded me to pursue my dreams, no matter the obstacles. Without your belief and cheering, stories like *Under the Sky, DFurious, Bound to the Lycan Prince & Kingsman* would never have come to life.

A special thanks to **Alberto Cruz Pérez**, who encouraged me to go for it, to start on my own, and to build everything from the ground up. Your words stayed with me and gave me the courage to trust the process—even when it felt overwhelming.

This is only the beginning.

If you'd like to explore more of my stories and upcoming projects, follow me on social media—I can't wait to share what's next with you.

Thank you for believing in these worlds and in me.

ABOUT THE AUTHOR

Liliz Black is a passionate storyteller from San Juan, Puerto Rico. Her love for reading and writing was sparked by the *Harry Potter* series, which also played a key role in helping her learn English. Bilingual in Spanish and English, she grew up imagining bold "what if" scenarios that later bloomed into full-fledged stories.

She began her writing journey with fanfiction before branching into original works, where she now builds complex universes that span romance, fantasy, drama, and dark intrigue. Under the name **Liliz Black**, she writes bold, emotional stories for adult audiences, while keeping **Yaniliz Negrón** for her family-friendly and children's projects.

She studied graphic design and game design at Atlantic College and currently lives in San Juan with her husband, their two children, two dogs, and seven cats. Whether she's designing, writing, or caring for her pets, creativity is at the heart of everything she does.

Follow her journey and dive into her worlds:

- **Instagram:** @lilizblack
- **Facebook:** @LBLilizBlack

Check out More